"You saw Izzy? Was she okay?"

Brayden hesitated, agitating her more. "Your nanny answered the door. She said Izzy was in bed, that she was sick."

Mila's pulse clamored. "But you didn't see her?"

He shook his head. "I'm afraid not."

Panic shot through her, and she dug her fingers into his arm. "I have to go to her, see her myself. Get her somewhere safe. Once DiSanti realizes what happened here today, he may hurt her or take her away somewhere."

Brayden nodded. "I'll tell Lucas where we're going."

"No," Mila cried. "Don't you understand? He has men at my house. They have guns. Izzy and I were video chatting when they burst in and took them hostage."

Brayden laid his hand over Mila's. The human contact felt comforting, and made her want to spill everything to him.

But she still had secrets.

Secrets she had to keep to protect her daughter.

HIDEAWAY AT HAWK'S LANDING

USA TODAY Bestselling Author

RITA HERRON

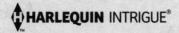

HARLEQUIN INTRIGUE®

To my wonderful daughter, Elizabeth, who helps real victims of domestic violence and human trafficking every day—you are amazing!

Love, Mom

ISBN-13: 978-1-335-52665-6

Hideaway at Hawk's Landing

Copyright © 2018 by Rita B. Herron

Recycling programs for this product may not exist in your area.

This edition published by arrangement with Harlequin Books S.A.

For questions and comments about the quality of this book, please contact us at CustomerService@Harlequin.com.

Printed in U.S.A.

www.Harlequin.com

USA TODAY bestselling author **Rita Herron** wrote her first book when she was twelve but didn't think real people grew up to be writers. Now she writes so she doesn't have to get a real job. A former kindergarten teacher and workshop leader, she traded storytelling to kids for writing romance, and now she writes romantic comedies and romantic suspense. Rita lives in Georgia with her family. She loves to hear from readers, so please visit her website, ritaherron.com.

Books by Rita Herron

Harlequin Intrigue

Badge of Justice

Redemption at Hawk's Landing
Hideaway at Hawk's Landing

The Heroes of Horseshoe Creek

Lock, Stock and McCullen
McCullen's Secret Son
Roping Ray McCullen
Warrior Son
The Missing McCullen
The Last McCullen

Cold Case at Camden Crossing
Cold Case at Carlton's Canyon
Cold Case at Cobra Creek
Cold Case in Cherokee Crossing

Visit the Author Profile page at Harlequin.com.

CAST OF CHARACTERS

Brayden Hawk—As a lawyer, he's known to fight for the underdog. As a Hawk, he knows what it's like to be loyal to his family—and to lose a child. As a man, he wants Mila Manchester. But how can he trust her when he senses she's holding back the truth?

Dr. Mila Manchester—Arrested for aiding and abetting a suspected human trafficker, she has to turn to Brayden Hawk for help. But keeping her secret about her daughter's father means lying to her lawyer.

Izzy Manchester—All three-year-old Izzy Manchester wants is to go home to her mommy. But some ruthless men are using her as a pawn to help Arman DiSanti escape the law.

Carina Welsch—A victim of DiSanti, she's running for her life, and for her child's.

Arman DiSanti—He trades and sells women and young girls like cattle. Can the Hawk men stop him and disband his operation?

Jorge—A cowboy who works for Lem Corley. Does he know where DiSanti and his men are hiding?

Lem Corley—Is this local cowboy involved in DiSanti's trafficking ring?

Jameson Beck—This councilman is a slick candidate for mayor, but is he hiding a connection to DiSanti?

Prologue

"Please, you have to take my baby." The young girl hid in the shadows of the awning, shivering as a dreary rain drizzled down, adding to the winter chill in the air.

Mila Manchester's heart ached for her. She knew her story. She was thirteen years old. Her name was Carina. Her mother had died in childbirth, and her father had abused her. Then he'd sold her to a man who used her as a sex slave.

Mila had helped Carina get to a shelter when she'd first escaped the monster.

Now Carina's slender pale face was shielded by a scarf, and her clothes were dark, allowing her to blend into the night.

A disguise.

She was terrified for her life.

The baby whimpered and Carina rocked her gently in her arms. "If he finds out little Isabella is his, he'll kill me and do God knows what with her."

Fear and grief laced the girl's voice. Carina was just a child herself. She should be in high school, hanging out with girlfriends, attending football games, shopping for dresses for the school dance.

Mila had wanted to report the situation to the police, but the girl had begged her not to. She'd confided about her pregnancy and claimed that the man didn't know. If he found out, he'd never let her go.

And if she went to the police, he *would* find out.

"Please, you're the only person I trust, Dr. Manchester. Promise me you'll give her a good life," the girl cried.

"Of course I will," Mila said. How could she turn her away? "But what about you? Do you want to stay with me—"

The girl shook her head, her eyes wild with panic. "No, he'll find me and kill both of us."

Mila's heart pounded. Unfortunately, she was right. "What will you do then?"

"I talked to those women at the shelter like you suggested. They know somebody who'll give me a new identity. They've even found me a place to stay so I can go to school."

So, the underground team was still operating. They'd helped so many abused women and children that she'd been afraid the police would shut them down.

Emotions clogged Mila's throat. This girl needed a chance to have a life. And so did the baby.

A noise sounded from the street, and the girl glanced over her shoulder. "They're waiting. This might be my only chance." She kissed the baby on the cheek. "I don't want you to think I'm a terrible mother—"

"I don't," Mila said. "It's obvious you love her, or you wouldn't have come here." But how could she take care of the child when she was just finishing her medical residency herself?

The girl suddenly threw herself against Mila and broke into a sob. Mila wrapped her arms around her and the infant and soothed her. "It's okay, sweetie. What happened to you isn't fair or right. You deserve to go to school and make a life for yourself."

The girl nodded against Mila, but she was crying and trembling as she turned and fled toward the waiting car.

Mila blinked back tears. She could take the child to the authorities. They'd find her a home. One with two parents.

But then she'd never know what happened to her…

And what if Carina came back one day looking for her daughter?

She looked down into the baby's sweet face. Her big eyes were watching her. Then the baby curled a tiny hand against Mila's breast.

Mila's heart melted. This baby needed her. She'd raise her as her own.

And she'd do anything to protect her.

Chapter One

Three years later

Having Isabella, Izzy, had changed Dr. Mila Manchester's life forever. She would do anything for her little girl.

Time to check in.

Mila ducked into the break room at the clinic where she worked and dialed her home number. When she was working, she missed Izzy, but they FaceTimed at least three times a day. And Izzy loved her nanny, Roberta, who'd been a Godsend to them both.

Izzy smiled up at her with big brown eyes. "Mommy, Mommy, Mommy!" Izzy twirled around the kitchen, her sparkling tiara bobbing sideways on her head.

"Look, Mommy, I'm a princess today."

"You're my little princess every day," Mila said with a smile.

Izzy pointed to the sequins on the pink dress Roberta had made for her. "Look, they sparkle."

"I see. I bet when the lights are off, you'll glow in the dark." Mila's heart swelled with love.

Izzy bobbed her head up and down. "That's what Bertie says," Izzy said. She had a difficult time saying Roberta's full name and had shortened it when she'd first started talking. Roberta didn't seem to mind.

Izzy raced over to the table and picked up a silver glittery wand. "Look, Bertie made this, too, so I can do magic."

"I can't wait to get home so you can show me your magic."

"Home?" Izzy ran around in circles. "Soon?"

"Mommy will be home in a little while." Mila's heart warmed at the sight of Roberta taking a pan of cookies from the oven. "Looks like you and Bertie are making yummy treats."

Roberta smiled from the bar, where she set the hot pan, and Izzy climbed up on the stool beside her. A bowl of chocolate frosting sat on the counter, and she jammed one finger in the bowl, scooped up a glob, then licked it off.

"Yummy!" Izzy squealed.

Mila rubbed her tummy with a grin. "Save me some, sweet girl."

Suddenly the back door into the kitchen at home flew open with a bang. Roberta startled and nearly dropped the second pan of cookies as two men in black stormed in, waving guns.

Mila clutched her phone, her heart pounding. "Roberta, Izzy—"

Roberta screamed and tucked Izzy close to her to protect her as one of the men aimed the semi at her. "Please, don't hurt us!" Roberta cried.

"Izzy, run!" Mila shouted.

But it was too late. Another bear of a man snatched Izzy.

"Put me down!" Izzy kicked and pounded the man's beefy arm with her fists.

He jerked her over his shoulder, then faced Mila. "Dr. Manchester, do what they tell you or you'll never see your daughter again."

They? What was he talking about?

Mila opened her mouth to plead with them, but a loud noise in the back of the clinic made her jump. She clutched her phone with clammy fingers and spun around as the door to the break room opened.

A man wearing all black stood in the doorway, a gun in his hand. "Get rid of the other people in the clinic and do it quietly."

She glanced at her screen again to see if Izzy was okay, but the call had ended. Panic shot through her. Battling the terror gripping her, she crossed her arms and struggled for calm. "You…have my daughter? Why?"

The man in black shrugged, thick brows puckering as he approached. "Do what we tell you and she won't get hurt."

Fear choked Mila. "What do you want?"

"You're going to give our leader a new face. Then we let your family go." He jerked her by the arm and shoved her toward the door. "Now, clear the clinic. The boss wants this done quickly and quietly."

"Who is your boss?"

"No names, Doc. It's better that way."

Mila sucked in a breath. "How do I know you'll keep your word and won't hurt Izzy?"

The man's cold eyes met hers. "You'll just have to trust us."

She didn't trust them at all.

He gestured toward the door, the gun aimed at her chest.

What else could she do? They had her daughter. She had no doubt they would hurt her if she didn't cooperate.

She stepped into the hallway and spotted one of her nurses frowning from the nurses' desk. She must have heard the noise.

"Unless you want her and your other staff to die, you'd better be quiet," the man growled behind her.

Mila nodded and stepped forward to get rid of her staff and the patients in the waiting room.

BRAYDEN HAWK WAS done with women. Especially with fix-ups.

His partner at the law firm, Conrad Barker, had told him Penny Lark was gorgeous. And she had been.

But he'd failed to point out that she had a hole in her head where her brain was supposed to be. That all she cared about was her beauty regime and money and being the focal point on the society page.

Of course, Conrad didn't care. He didn't date women for their brains or because he wanted a future with them. He simply wanted sex.

Tension eased from Brayden as he drove onto Hawk's Landing, the family ranch. The wind whistled through the windows of his SUV, trees swaying slightly in the late fall breeze.

At one time he'd been like Conrad. Not that he
wanted a woman for her money, but he hadn't wanted
a relationship either.

The last few months with his family had changed
everything.

For nearly two decades, the ranch had been a sad,
lonely reminder of his missing little sister, Chrissy. And
also of the fact that his father had deserted them shortly
after her disappearance.

Thankfully, Chrissy's murder had finally been solved
and the family had closure.

Shortly after, his oldest brother, Harrison, the sheriff
of Tumbleweed, had married Honey Granger.

And a few weeks ago, the next to the oldest brother,
Lucas, an FBI agent, had married Charlotte Reacher, a
victim in a shooting by a human trafficking ring Lucas
was investigating.

On the heels of adding two wives to the family, his
mother had opened the ranch to four foster girls, Charlotte's art students, who'd needed a home after Lucas
had rescued them from the trafficking ring, an operation known as Shetland.

Unfortunately, the ringleader of the operation had
escaped and was in the wind.

And now Honey was pregnant, due in just a few
weeks, and the house was alive again with family, with
talk of babies and the next generation of Hawks.

Odd how that conversation had sparked thoughts of
settling down himself.

Brayden shook off the thought, climbed from the
SUV, smiling at the sound of the horses galloping on
the hill. Since the girls had moved in, they'd added

more livestock, and he'd hired his friend Beau Fortner as foreman of the ranch operation.

His mother swept him into a hug as he entered the foyer. "So glad you made it to dinner, Brayden."

"I wouldn't miss it, Mom." The weekly family get-togethers had meant a lot to his mother during the lean years.

Truth be told, it had meant a lot to him, too. He'd harbored guilt over his sister's disappearance and had needed his family around him.

Charlotte and Honey and the girls were laying out a spread of food that would feed half of Texas while Lucas, Harrison and brother number three, Dexter, stood by the sideboard sipping scotch. Dexter handed him a highball glass, and Brayden inhaled the rich aroma before taking a sip.

"Thanks, I needed this."

"Bad day in court?" Lucas asked.

Brayden shrugged. He would have rather been in court than on that damn date. Thank God it had only been lunch.

His mother called them to the table, and they gathered for the blessing, then the meal. Excited talk of the nursery Honey was putting together for baby Hawk floated between the women while Dexter filled them in on the new horses he'd bought.

Lucas's phone buzzed with a text, earning a chiding look from his mother. She respected all their jobs but insisted they leave their phones and business at the door.

"Sorry, Mom," Lucas murmured. "It's about the Shetland operation."

The room grew quiet. Strained.

Lucas stood and walked to the foyer away from the table. Harrison followed. Tension stretched into a pained silence as they waited to find out if the Shetland ring had struck again.

MILA SWALLOWED BACK the terror clawing at her as she approached the head nurse in the clinic.

"Rhoda, will you please tell everyone to leave? I have to get home to Izzy. She's sick."

Rhoda gave her a worried look. "Is she okay?"

Mila fought a sob, then nodded. "She will be, but she needs her mommy. Just send the patients home and we'll reschedule." She squeezed Rhoda's arm. "You go home, too. I'll close up."

Rhoda was a single mother with a ten-year-old son at home, so she didn't mind an opportunity to take off early.

Mila felt the gunman's eyes piercing her as she watched Rhoda quickly clear the waiting room, then shut down the computer at the nurses' desk.

"Anything else I can do?" Rhoda called from the front.

"No, thanks for handling that. Have a good night with Trey."

Rhoda yelled good-night, then left through the front door.

The gunman motioned for her to lock up, and Mila rushed forward, locked the doors and closed all the blinds. Noises sounded from the back, and she walked toward the exam rooms on shaky legs.

"Why me? Why here?" Mila asked.

The gunman jabbed the gun into her back. "We know you helped some of our girls escape."

A cold chill washed over Mila. Some of their girls?

She had referred a few lost teens at the clinic to the women's shelter. And then there was Izzy's mother…

The back door burst open, and four more armed men strode in, their big bodies shielding another man in a suit who she assumed was the boss.

The guards scanned the interior, their posture braced to shoot. As they parted to search the clinic to make sure they were alone, she got her first real look at the man they called their leader.

Thick black hair framed an angular face that might be handsome if not for the scar running down the side of his cheek and the evil in his black eyes.

Eyes that looked familiar.

Pure panic robbed her breath.

She knew who he was. Arman DiSanti—the man who'd bought and used Izzy's mother as a sex slave.

Did he know that her daughter, Izzy, the little girl they'd taken hostage, was his birth child?

BRAYDEN TRIED TO keep everyone calm as they waited on Lucas to answer the phone call. When Lucas returned, he looked antsy.

"We have a lead on the ringleader of the Shetland operation. We think he's undergoing cosmetic surgery to change his identity." He pulled his keys from his pocket. "I have to go."

Harrison leaned over to give Honey a kiss. "I'm going with him."

As sheriff of Tumbleweed, Harrison had no jurisdiction outside their small town, but he'd caught the case when Charlotte had been shot during the abductions of four students from her art studio. Lucas had been called in then. At this point, the entire family and the girls were all invested in making sure the trafficking ring was shut down for good.

"Need backup?" Dexter asked.

Dex's PI skills had come in handy when they'd been tracking down the missing girls.

Lucas shook his head no. "This is an FBI operation, but thanks."

Charlotte stood and touched her husband's arm. "Where are you going?"

"A clinic outside Austin. Some plastic surgeon named Dr. Manchester is giving the bastard a new face."

Charlotte's eyes widened. "Dr. Manchester?"

Lucas nodded. "Mila Manchester. For all we know, she's on Shetland's payroll. Her volunteer work could be a cover to give her opportunities to do jobs like this."

Charlotte shook her head. "No, Lucas. Mila can't be involved."

Lucas narrowed his eyes at his wife. "You know Dr. Manchester?"

She nodded. "Her mother is the doctor who removed my port-wine birthmark when I was younger. I met Mila when I was at the clinic. And I've read about her volunteer work. She's a good person."

Lucas glanced at the table, where everyone was watching. Fear darkened the teens' faces while worry knitted his mother's brow.

"Maybe you think you know her," Lucas said. "But,

Charlotte, these men could be paying her big money to help them."

Charlotte shook her head in denial again. "No, not Mila. She's kind and loving and giving just like her mother was."

Lucas looked torn but dropped a kiss on Charlotte's cheek. "I really have to go. We don't want this guy to get away."

"Be careful," Charlotte said, her voice strained. "And promise me you won't hurt Mila."

Lucas hugged her tightly. "Everything will be okay."

Brayden pushed back from the table and followed Lucas and Harrison to the door. Dexter was right behind him.

Lucas stepped outside. "I'll call you when we have him in custody."

Brayden nodded. "Just get the bastard."

Chapter Two

Mila typically took weeks to plan a facial reconstruction surgery. She had several consultations with the patient, conducted an analysis of problematic features needing correction, created computer sketches simulating what the finished product would look like and, if needed, arranged counseling with a professional. She'd also run blood work and tests to verify the patient was healthy enough for surgery.

Sometimes skin grafts were necessary. And sometimes multiple surgeries.

She had no time for any of that today.

DiSanti had shoved a photograph into her hands and told her exactly what he'd wanted. The changes would literally make him unrecognizable.

She'd been working for hours now. Her hand trembled as she finished the last of the sutures around his forehead. Perspiration trickled down the side of her face. Exhaustion bled through every cell in her body, adding to the tension thrumming through her. Her feet ached, her head throbbed and her eyes were blurring.

Twice his blood pressure had risen, and she'd thought she might lose him. That would be a blessing.

But the guards had warned her that if she made a mistake or if he died, she'd pay for it.

"How much longer?" the shortest of the guards asked.

"I'm almost finished. But he's going to need recovery time." She wanted to tell them they were fools to put him through so many alterations in one day. "I told you that I usually perform these procedures in steps."

"We don't have time for that," the bigger brute barked. "Just finish."

Images of Izzy and Roberta, terrified for their lives, taunted her with every minute she worked on the man. So far, she'd reshaped his nose, lifted his eyelids and added fillers to his cheeks and lips. His scar was history, as well.

He looked ten years younger and almost handsome.

But nothing could change the monster beneath that face.

The goons guarding the surgical room remained rigid, guns pointing at her.

Her finger slipped, and she bit her tongue as she dropped the instrument. The guard took a step forward, his glare a warning. If she lost DiSanti, she'd be dead in seconds.

She forced a breath to calm her nerves, then completed the row of stitches, dabbing away blood as she went.

Relieved to finally finish, she gestured toward her patient. "He's going to need rest, ice packs, pain medication. I'll send you with everything you need to take care of him."

A snide grin slid onto the brute's face. "We're not going to take care of him, Doc. You are."

Mila's pulse pounded. "Listen, I did everything you asked. Now let me go home to my little girl."

He shook his head. "Not happening yet. Not until he's healing and we know you didn't pull something on us."

The shorter man's phone buzzed. He stepped aside to answer, then spoke in a low hushed voice. Anger slashed his eyes as he hung up. "We have to move him now. The feds are on their way."

Mila gripped the steel counter where her instruments were spread out. If the feds were coming, maybe they'd save Izzy.

The men jumped into motion. Keeping the IV attached, they rolled the patient through the hallway and loaded him into the back of their van. The bigger guy jerked her arm. "Come on, Doc. Get whatever supplies you need to take care of him and let's go."

She dug her heels in. "Please let me go home to my daughter. I'll gather the supplies and you can take them with you."

He jammed the gun at her temple. "I said move it."

A siren wailed outside. One of the guards rushed in. "We have to go now. The damn feds are here!"

The man dragged her into the hall. She pulled back, desperate to escape. If they took her with them, they'd probably kill her and she'd never see Izzy again.

But the barrel of the gun pressed into her temple. "Fight and I'll kill you right here."

The siren wailed closer. No time to get supplies.

Mila fought a sob as the man dragged her out the back door.

Tires screeched. An SUV careened into the parking lot, a police car following. Blue lights twirled and flickered against the night sky.

Car doors opened, and a man shouted, "Stop, FBI!"

Two of the guards at the back of the van opened fire and men ducked for cover.

The man holding her arm lost his grip and fired back, then motioned for the two guards to get in the van. They jumped inside, while another one rushed into the driver's seat. The engine roared to life, then shouts and bullets flew.

The big guy shoved her toward the van, but she kicked him in the knee. He cursed and pushed her again, but she dived to the side and hit the concrete. Another round of bullets pinged around her, then the big guy jumped inside the vehicle.

Mila covered her head with her hands as the FBI fired at the van. Through the back window the guards unleashed another round.

She screamed as a bullet pinged onto the concrete by her face.

Tires peeled rubber as the van screeched away. Footsteps and shouts followed. The officers were leaving. She raised her head to look around, but a tall, dark-haired man stood over her, his gun aimed at her.

"Dr. Manchester?"

She nodded, her body trembling.

He hauled her to her feet. "You are under arrest."

She opened her mouth to protest. But he spun her around, yanked her arms behind her and snapped hand-cuffs around her wrists.

KEEPING THE HAWK women calm was an impossible job.

Brayden and Dexter tried everything from encouraging the girls to talk about riding to feigning interest in the plans for Honey's nursery.

The fact that Honey didn't want to talk about the baby's room was not a good sign.

Charlotte paced in front of the fireplace in the den, where they'd gathered to have coffee and the blueberry cobbler his mother had baked. But no one was hungry and everyone wanted drinks instead of coffee. Except for Honey, of course.

"I wish they'd call," Charlotte said as she made the turn at the corner of the fireplace for the dozenth time.

"Harrison has to come back okay." Honey rubbed her growing belly. "This little boy needs his daddy."

An awkward silence followed as her comment hit too close to home. He and his brothers had needed their father, but he'd left and never contacted them again.

"I'm sorry," Honey said. "That was insensitive."

"It's the truth." Their mother patted Honey's shoulder. "We are not keeping secrets or mincing words. Your baby needs Harrison, and he's coming back to you both."

Brayden's phone buzzed, and everyone startled.

"Is it Lucas?" Charlotte asked at the same time Honey asked if it was Harrison.

He checked the number. "Harrison." He quickly connected, then listened.

"I don't have much time. Arman DiSanti was at the clinic in Austin, but he escaped. Two FBI agents chased after him but lost him on the outskirts of Austin. We have an APB out for the van and have alerted all authorities."

The women were boring holes into him with their anxious expressions. "Are you and Lucas all right?" Brayden asked.

"Yeah," Harrison said. "Lucas arrested Dr. Manchester. We're transporting her to the field office here in Austin for questioning. Tell Honey to go home and get some rest. I'll be home later."

Brayden frowned. "I will."

As soon as he hung up, Charlotte and Honey pounced on him. "What happened? Are they okay?"

"Lucas and Harrison are safe. Unfortunately, DiSanti escaped." Brayden glanced at Honey. "Harrison said for you to go home and rest."

Honey released a sigh of relief. "I know he loves what he does, but I can't help but worry."

Charlotte put her arm around Honey. "Me, too. Every time Lucas leaves the house, I say a prayer that he'll come back in one piece."

Mrs. Hawk clapped her hands. "Well, now that we know our men are safe, how about that pie?"

Honey rubbed her stomach again. "I don't think so, but thanks."

Dexter went for it, but Charlotte declined, then cornered him by the fireplace. "What happened with Mila?"

Brayden reached for the bottle of scotch to pour another drink. He'd held off while they waited, deciding he needed to remain sober in case there was an emergency. He'd only served on the police force a year before deciding on law school, but he knew how dangerous the streets were.

"Brayden, tell me," Charlotte said, an urgency to her voice that made him step away from the bar.

"Lucas arrested her. They're taking her to the field office in Austin for questioning."

Charlotte's face crumpled. "I'm going. I have to see her."

She rushed toward the coat rack in the foyer and retrieved her purse. Brayden hurried after her.

"Wait, Charlotte, I'm sure Lucas will call you."

"He arrested her," Charlotte said. "That's not right. I know Mila wouldn't help those men."

"Apparently, she did," Brayden said. "They were at her clinic."

Charlotte shook her head vigorously. "No. There's more to the story. And she's going to need a lawyer."

Brayden threw up his hands. He didn't want to get in the middle of an argument between Charlotte and his brother.

"Please," Charlotte said. "Go with me and listen to what she has to say."

Her pleading tone sucker punched him. He didn't know Mila Manchester. But he did know Charlotte, and his brother's wife was one of the most honest, caring women he'd ever met.

He tugged his keys from his pocket. "All right, I'll drive you. But I'm not promising anything."

He explained the situation to the family and agreed to keep them posted, then escorted Charlotte to his SUV. Her shaky breathing rattled in the SUV as he drove from the ranch onto the road through town, then to the highway leading to Austin.

"Tell me about this Dr. Manchester," he said as he sped around traffic.

She retrieved a photo of the doctor on her phone. His gut pinched.

Mila Manchester was a plastic surgeon—but she could have passed for a model. Well, maybe not a model. She wasn't rail thin or gaunt-looking or covered in layers of makeup.

Instead she was naturally beautiful. Huge dark eyes stood out against ivory skin and pale pink lips. Her hair was a fiery dark color with streaks of red.

There was also a softness about her that made her look wholesome.

He jerked his eyes back to the road. He couldn't get distracted by her good looks. Sometimes the lookers were shallow beneath.

Charlotte twisted her hands together. "I was born with a port-wine birthmark," Charlotte said. "No one wanted to adopt me because of it. Dr. Manchester, Mila's mother, did volunteer work and removed it for me at no cost." She paused, her voice warbling. "I met Mila the day before the surgery. She was about my age but wasn't turned off by the way I looked. I guess she'd seen worse at her mother's practice."

"Her mother sounds like a saint."

"She was," Charlotte said. "I owe so much to her. And Mila. She visited me every day at the clinic while I healed. She told me she wanted to be like her mother."

Her story was getting to Brayden. "And you think she is?"

Charlotte nodded. "I've read about her work. She's generous and caring and volunteers with Doctors Without Borders... There's no way she'd help the Shetland operation hurt innocent girls."

Brayden hoped she was right. Lucas's wife had been through enough without learning that her friend was a criminal.

They lapsed into silence until they reached Austin and the field office. As they parked and walked in, Charlotte grew more jittery.

Lucas was probably going to kill him for bringing her.

But her description of the doctor had piqued his curiosity.

Harrison met them at the front door.

"Lucas is about to question her," Harrison said.

"I'd like to observe," Brayden said.

Harrison frowned but glanced at Charlotte and seemed to realize Brayden was trying to appease Lucas's wife. He ushered them through security, then to a room with a viewing screen to watch the interrogation.

Brayden's gut tightened as Lucas appeared, his hand on Dr. Manchester's arm.

Damn. Even with her long dark hair tangled and escaping a haphazard ponytail, her clothes disheveled, and her face pale and exhausted-looking, she was stunning.

She heaved a weary breath and looked up at the camera in the corner as if she knew it was there. But she didn't make a move to fix her hair or put on pretenses.

Instead her big brown eyes were haunted and filled with fear.

Fear that made him want to find out the truth about what had happened today. Was she helping the Shetland operation?

Chapter Three

Mila fought tears, but they streamed down her face as Special Agent Lucas Hawk escorted her into an interrogation room.

He'd been careful to explain where they were and that she was in federal custody.

She didn't know what to do. Didn't know if Izzy and Roberta were dead or alive.

Pain mingled with panic at the thought.

If she talked, those terrible men would hurt Izzy.

Agent Hawk placed a bottle of water on the hard surface of the table in the room. She'd seen enough crime shows to know that she was being watched. That they'd record whatever she said. That they'd get her prints from the water bottle.

Sweat beaded on her upper lip and forehead, trickling into her hair.

It had been hours since she'd eaten or drunk anything. Hours since those men had broken in and threatened her. Hours since she'd started the surgeries that would enable that monster to escape.

Agent Hawk was watching her with steely eyes. Another agent named Hoover stood by the door, his arms folded, expression condescending as if he'd already tried and convicted her.

Agent Hawk's boots clicked on the hard floor as he crossed the room. He narrowed his eyes at her as if dissecting her, then removed a key from his pocket and uncuffed her hands.

She breathed out, grateful to be free of the heavy metal on her wrists so she could reach the water. Feeling dehydrated, she turned up the bottle and drank half of it in one long gulp.

Water trickled down her chin, and she wiped at it, then glanced at her fingers. Even though she'd worn gloves during the surgery, the stench of the ugly man's blood lingered.

"Dr. Manchester," Agent Hawk began. "You know the reason you're here?"

She nodded, then looked up at him, but she couldn't stand the accusations in his eyes, so she jerked her gaze back to her hands.

He slapped a photograph of Arman DiSanti onto the table. "You performed plastic surgery on this man today at your clinic?"

She chewed her bottom lip. He knew that or he wouldn't have arrested her.

"Answer me," he said, his tone cold.

She gave a slight nod. What good would a lie do when he'd practically caught her red-handed?

"Arman DiSanti is the man we suspect to be the ringleader of a human trafficking ring called the Shetland operation," Agent Hawk said bluntly. "This group has abducted dozens of teenage girls in Texas this past year."

She willed herself not to react. But Izzy's sweet face crying as that man snatched her taunted her. Where was her little girl now?

The agent paced in front of her, then spread several pictures on the table. "These are photographs of some of the teens abducted this year. At least these are the ones we rescued." He named each girl, then pinned her with an accusatory look as if she was responsible. "No telling how many more victims he's had kidnapped."

She swallowed back bile. She knew what a horrid man he was. That was the reason she'd taken Izzy from her mother to raise her.

The agent laid another photo on the table then another and another. The first one showed a dark building with a cage in it. Blood dotted the floor.

Another photo revealed pictures of chains attached to a pole. Then another yielded a close-up of the words *Help us* crudely etched into the wall.

"He chained them to the wall and locked them in a cage like they were animals." The next picture showed two young teens dressed skimpily as they stood in front of what appeared to be a camera. Both girls were glassy-eyed, drugged.

"Then he sells them at an auction like they're cattle. That's where he got the name Shetland for his operation." He tapped DiSanti's photograph. "This is the man you helped escape the law today, Dr. Manchester." He slapped one more picture on the table, this one of a dead girl, her skeletal figure decaying.

Mila bit back a gasp.

"This is a girl named Louise Summerton. She was murdered when she tried to escape the man who bought her."

Nausea welled in Mila's stomach.

She fought it, but her stomach heaved. Panicked, she covered her mouth, her chest convulsing. The agent at the door must have realized she was going to throw up because he grabbed a trash can and shoved it in front of her.

Emotions overcame her, and tears rained down her face as she retched into the trash can.

BRAYDEN BROKE OUT in a sweat as he watched Mila Manchester purge the contents of her stomach.

"Look at her," Charlotte cried. "Something's terribly wrong, Brayden. Tell Lucas to stop this right now. I want to see Mila."

Brayden gritted his teeth. Lucas was not going to allow that, not until he was satisfied he'd gleaned all the information from Dr. Manchester that he could. He'd been trained in interrogation techniques, taught not to allow emotions to interfere when questioning a suspect.

They'd both also been taught how to read body language. And this woman's body language screamed that she was frightened.

Charlotte reached for the doorknob, but Brayden placed a hand over hers. "Let me handle it."

Tears blurred Charlotte's eyes as she looked at him. "She didn't do this, Brayden. Tell Lucas I know she's innocent."

Except she had operated on the man. Had given him a new face.

She hadn't denied that.

Charlotte lifted her chin. "Tell Lucas I hired you to represent Mila."

Oh boy. That was not going to go over well.

"I don't want to come between you and Lucas—"

"You won't," Charlotte said. "But I have to do what's right. Mila and her mother helped so many people that it's time someone helped Mila."

Maybe she was right.

He stepped into the hallway. Harrison met him, his expression concerned. "Deputy outside Austin spotted the van, but men shot at him, and he lost them. Looks like they're headed west."

"Let's pray they catch them," Charlotte said from behind him.

Harrison nodded. "Did Dr. Manchester give Lucas any information?"

Brayden shook his head. "Not yet."

"I hired Brayden to represent her," Charlotte said in a tone that brooked no argument. "Maybe she'll confide in him."

Harrison's frown was exactly the reaction Brayden expected.

"Tell Lucas I want to talk to her," he said.

"Brayden—"

"Tell him," Charlotte said. "Or I'll go in there and tell him myself."

Brayden fought a tiny smile. Lucas said the woman had spunk. He was right.

Harrison grunted, then gestured for them to follow him, and a minute later, he knocked on the interrogation room, then poked his head in. "Lucas, a word please."

Lucas joined them in the hallway, took one look at Charlotte and grimaced. "You should have stayed home."

Charlotte folded her arms. "I couldn't. I know Mila, and she's innocent."

"We have proof," Lucas said.

Brayden cleared his throat. "Let me talk to her."

"This is an interrogation, Brayden. We're trying to find the man who runs the Shetland ring." He aimed a look at Charlotte. "You do want him to be arrested, don't you? Because he will keep trafficking young girls unless we stop him."

"Of course I want him to be stopped," Charlotte said, her eyes widening in anger and surprise that Lucas would suggest she didn't.

"Maybe you should let Brayden try," Harrison said. "She might talk to him."

Lucas glared at Harrison. "If he speaks to her as her lawyer, he's bound by attorney-client privilege. What good will that do us?"

Brayden squared his shoulders. "Listen, Lucas, I'll find out the truth. If I think she intentionally helped the Shetland group, I won't represent her." He gestured toward the closed door. "But I was watching what happened in there. She looks terrified. She couldn't fake that kind of reaction when she saw those pictures."

Lucas stood ramrod straight. "Give me another minute. If she doesn't offer anything, then you can come in."

Brayden agreed, and Lucas disappeared inside again. He and Harrison and Charlotte returned to the room to watch the interview.

Mila was wiping her face with a paper towel. She looked pale and fatigued and on the verge of a breakdown.

"Dr. Manchester," Lucas said in a quiet but firm tone.

"We know you performed plastic surgery on DiSanti. We just don't know why you helped him."

Mila rubbed her forehead, a sound of anguish coming from her, but she didn't reply.

"We understand that DiSanti will need time to recover from the surgery. He's well guarded by his pit bulls. Where were they taking him?"

Mila's lower lip quivered. "I don't know."

Lucas's jaw snapped tight. "If we don't stop him, he'll kidnap more young girls." Again, Lucas tapped the photos one by one, his tone full of disgust. "More innocent girls who will be turned into sex slaves to build his empire and pad his fortune."

Mila stared at the pictures, ashen faced.

"Where were they going?" Lucas pressed.

Misery darkened Mila's expression as she looked up at Lucas. "I don't know. I honestly don't."

Lucas stared at her for a long minute, then swiped the photographs into a stack, jammed them in an envelope and stalked from the room.

Brayden rushed to meet him in the hall, Harrison and Charlotte on his heels.

"All right, see what you can do," Lucas said. "Finding DiSanti is what matters. Tell her we'll offer her a deal if she talks."

Brayden reached for the door.

"I hope to hell you're right about her," he heard Lucas tell Charlotte just before he stepped inside the room.

One look into Mila's tormented eyes, and Brayden had to remind himself to be neutral. Beautiful women lied and deceived people all the time.

He had to convince her to tell him the truth. That was all that mattered. That and putting the Shetland ring out of business.

MILA TWISTED HER hands together, fighting another wave of nausea. More than anything, she wanted to tell Agent Hawk what was happening. To beg him to send someone to her house and check on Izzy and the nanny.

But if she did and DiSanti found out, they might hurt Izzy. Her stomach knotted. What if they'd already taken her somewhere?

Panic clawed at her insides. The door opened again, and the agent appeared, but this time another man stood beside him. He was also tall, broad shouldered, muscular, with thick dark hair. They had the same dark brows.

"Dr. Manchester, this is Brayden Hawk. He's an attorney who my wife hired to represent you."

Mila stared at them in confusion. "Excuse me?"

"My wife is Charlotte Reacher," Agent Hawk said. "She's outside and insists you have counsel."

"Charlotte—is your wife?"

"Yes. We met when she was shot by DiSanti's men."

Oh God, that was right. She'd seen the news story. No wonder this man was out to get DiSanti. It was personal.

But he was allowing her an attorney…

Or was it a trap?

It struck her then—the attorney's last name was Hawk just as the agent's was. Were they related?

She scrutinized the men's features. Yes, they had to be brothers.

Agent Hawk gave his brother a dark look, then slipped from the room. Mila's head was spinning.

The lawyer cleared his throat. "Dr. Manchester, I know you've been through hell today. I'd like to hear your side of the story."

Mila's lungs squeezed for air. Was he really here to help her?

Could she trust him with the truth, or would telling him about her daughter being held hostage put Izzy in more danger?

Chapter Four

Brayden studied Mila as Lucas left the interrogation room. Some clients were desperate enough to pour out their story immediately.

Others took finessing. Especially if they were afraid.

And this woman was frightened of something…

Hoping to put her ease, he claimed the chair across from her and adopted a soothing voice. "Dr. Manchester, I agreed to talk to you because Charlotte is concerned about you." He softened his voice. "She believes in you, and Lucas and I both believe in Charlotte."

The woman's face twisted with emotions.

"Anything you tell me is confidential. But if I'm going to represent you, you need to explain your side of the story."

She rubbed her forehead, then looked down at her hands on the table.

"Please talk to me," Brayden said quietly.

Dr. Manchester sighed warily. "I already told you that I don't know where they were taking DiSanti."

Brayden let the silence stretch for a moment. "They didn't mention a city or town?"

She shook her head no. "I'm sorry. I...don't know what else to tell you."

"Stop giving me the runaround," Brayden said, his voice firmer. "Did you know who DiSanti was when you performed plastic surgery on him?"

Fear flashed in her eyes.

"You did," he said, reading her reaction. "But you helped him anyway."

She averted her gaze, then massaged her forehead again with a shaky hand.

"We know DiSanti has amassed a fortune," he continued. "Is that the reason you did it? For the money?"

Her troubled gaze jerked to his, but she bit her lip and didn't answer.

"Charlotte insists you do good work, that you donate your time and expertise to help people, especially children, in trouble." He raised a brow. "That description doesn't fit with you giving someone like DiSanti a new identity."

Dr. Manchester pressed a fist to her mouth and breathed heavily.

"Help me out here, Doc. I'm trying to understand."

"No one can understand," Dr. Manchester said, a warble to her voice.

"I might if you talk to me." Dammit, he wanted to believe her. Wanted her to be the person Charlotte described.

"Did he donate money to the clinic in exchange for a new face?"

She shook her head, misery darkening her eyes.

Brayden's patience was wearing thin. "Did you owe him for some reason?"

She twisted her hands together.

"Come on, Dr. Manchester, I can't help you if you don't confide in me." He racked his brain for answers, then it hit him. "You're afraid. Did DiSanti and his people threaten you?"

MILA WANTED TO spill the entire story and assure him that she despised DiSanti and his men, that she'd never do anything to help them. That the entire time she'd been operating on him she'd felt sick to her stomach.

Most of all, she wanted to beg Brayden Hawk to check on her daughter.

But what if DiSanti's men were watching?

According to the news, the police suspected DiSanti had a local contact in Tumbleweed. Who knew how many he had in Austin?

Or who they were. He might have contacts right here in the FBI or at the local police department.

She didn't know whom to trust.

Brayden leaned across the table and pierced her with those blue eyes, eyes that were ice-cold. "Talk to me, Doc."

She chose her words carefully. "I wish I could tell you what you want to hear, Mr. Hawk, but I can't."

He cleared his throat. "Please call me Brayden. If you're concerned I'll tell the FBI, you don't have to be. As your attorney, I'm bound by attorney-client privilege."

Maybe she should talk to him. If he understood, he'd send someone to see if Izzy was okay. "He's your brother. How do I know this isn't a trap?"

The ice in his eyes hardened. "Because I'm a man

of my word. I chose law to help people." He leaned closer. "And I think you're scared and that you need a friend right now."

Emotions swelled inside her at the compassion in his voice.

She opened her mouth to speak, but the door opened and Agent Hawk appeared again. This time another man in an expensive three-piece suit stood beside him. "Excuse me," Agent Hawk said, "but Mr. Polk, Dr. Manchester's attorney, is here."

The suited man strode into the room, his skin pale, his dark glare intimidating. "Dr. Manchester, don't say another word."

Mila bit her lip. Brayden Hawk frowned and glanced at the man, then back at her. Suspicion took root in his expression, then a flash of anger.

She gripped the chair edge with sweaty fingers.

"Dr. Manchester, is Mr. Polk your attorney?" Brayden asked.

Mila barely stifled a scream of protest. But the attorney shot her a warning look, and she refrained.

"Is he your attorney?" Agent Hawk asked.

She blinked back tears and nodded. But she couldn't look at Brayden. She had a bad feeling that Polk worked for DiSanti and Brayden knew it.

Worse, he hadn't come to help her. He'd come to make sure she kept her mouth shut about DiSanti.

Brayden stood, shoulders rigid, debating how to handle the situation. Dammit, he'd been making headway with Mila Manchester until this lawyer showed up. He'd seen the agony on her face when she'd looked at those pictures and was inclined to believe Charlotte.

Dr. Manchester had been coerced into performing surgery on DiSanti. That was the only explanation that fit.

And he had no doubt that Polk had been sent by DiSanti to protect DiSanti's interests.

Mila looked terrified of the man.

He didn't want to leave her alone with him, but unless she spoke up, he'd have to.

Lucas cleared his throat. "We'll let you talk."

He opened the door and gestured for Brayden to leave.

"What the hell?" Brayden said as they walked down the hall.

Lucas ushered him into a small office next to the interrogation room.

"You know that man is not her attorney," Brayden said. "DiSanti sent him to keep her from talking."

Lucas ran a hand through his hair. "Probably so. But unless she orders him to get lost or decides to answer our questions, there's not a damn thing I can do about it."

He and his brother locked stubborn gazes. "Can't you charge Polk with being an accomplice or something?"

Lucas gave him a wry look. "Not without probable cause or evidence. And we have nothing on the man."

"Then find something," Brayden said. "Because you can't leave Mila alone with him or release her in his custody. He may be the one threatening her."

Lucas narrowed his eyes. "Did she tell you that she was threatened?"

Brayden clamped his mouth closed, frustrated. She hadn't actually said so, but he'd seen the fear in her eyes.

"You know I can't divulge anything she revealed to me in private."

"Right." Their gazes locked again, both at a standstill.

Brayden pasted on his poker face. If he wanted Mila to trust him, he had to prove he was trustworthy.

And that meant honoring Mila's confidence.

If he'd only had five more minutes with her...

"What are you going to do?" Brayden asked his brother.

Lucas scowled. "Find out everything I can on Polk before tomorrow."

"What about tonight?" Brayden asked.

"She'll have to spend the night locked up," Lucas said. "Maybe some time in a cell will persuade her to talk. If not, and Polk returns tomorrow to bail her out, I'll have to release her."

"She'll face charges?"

Lucas nodded. "Yes. It may be the only leverage we have."

God, he hated to see Mila Manchester spend the night in jail. But at least she'd be safe from that bastard DiSanti.

Meanwhile, maybe Lucas could dig up some dirt on Polk, hopefully enough to arrest him and keep him away from Mila.

MILA'S STOMACH KNOTTED as Polk settled into the chair across from her. His tight lips and beady eyes made her want to scream for help from Brayden Hawk.

At least she'd thought Brayden was sincere.

She'd promised to raise Izzy and keep her safe, but she couldn't do that in prison.

"You work for him, don't you?" she asked in a low whisper.

A sinister smile crept onto his face. "What did you tell them?"

She guessed that was her answer. "Nothing."

His thick brows shot up. "Nothing? Are you sure?"

"I'm sure," she said. "I have no idea how they learned he was at my clinic."

"You didn't tip off that nurse to call them?"

"No." Anger made her voice hard. "I did exactly what I was told. Now, where is my daughter? Is she safe?"

He made a low sound in his throat. "What did you think would happen to her when you tried to escape at the clinic?"

Her stomach roiled, tears choking her. She shook her head in denial. They couldn't have hurt her little girl; she had to be all right. Izzy was her whole life.

"Where is she?" she said through gritted teeth. "Did your people hurt her? Because if you did, what's to stop me from talking to the FBI?"

"Now, now, just calm down," the man said in a condescending tone. "Your daughter is safe. At least for now."

Her breath rushed out. She hated this man and Di-Santi with every fiber of her being. "She's an innocent little girl," Mila whispered. "Please don't harm her. She has nothing to do with this."

"But she's important to you," Polk said sharply. "So,

if you want her to celebrate her next birthday, then you'll cooperate."

"I already did," Mila said. "I performed the damn surgery. DiSanti has his new face, so leave me and my daughter alone."

"You said yourself that there's a risk of infection. Your services may be needed for recovery."

He stood, and ran his hand over his diamond-chip tie clip. "I will be back tomorrow to post bond. Meanwhile, you are not to tell anyone about our conversation. And you won't discuss DiSanti."

He strode to the door and turned back to face her, his look ominous. "Remember what I said. Your daughter has lovely eyes and hair, Dr. Manchester. And a perfect face for now. Wouldn't you hate for something to happen to change that?"

Cold terror shot through Mila. She pressed her hand over her mouth to stifle a scream as he walked out and shut the door behind him.

BRAYDEN DID NOT want to leave Mila locked up in that cell tonight. For all they knew, DiSanti had someone on the inside who might try to hurt her to keep her from talking.

Unless Polk had threatened her into silence.

"Let me talk to her one more time," he said to Lucas.

"She has an attorney," Lucas said tightly. "And you seem to be forgetting that she's a criminal."

"Not if she was coerced." Brayden gritted his teeth. "For God sakes, Lucas, don't be such a hard-ass. Your own wife asked me to represent her."

"I'm doing this for my wife and those girls at Mother's

and all the other teens and women DiSanti has forced into sexual slavery."

Brayden silently counted to ten to gather his composure. On the surface, he knew Lucas was right.

But there were extenuating circumstances.

"She was on the verge of talking to me," Brayden said. "Give me one more shot."

A muscle ticked in his brother's jaw. "All right. Five minutes. But then I take her to a holding cell. Maybe a night in lockup will persuade her she needs to come clean."

Brayden agreed. What else could he do?

Lucas escorted him to the interrogation room, his expression grim. If she agreed to accept Polk's help as her attorney, his brother's hands were tied, too.

Brayden forced a neutral expression as he entered the room. The moment he saw the tears in Mila's eyes though, he nearly lost it.

Ever since he'd represented his friend, who'd been wrongly convicted, and gotten him off, he'd earned a reputation for fighting for the underdog.

Mila Manchester might be fooling him. Those tears could be due to the fact that she was upset about getting caught.

Or they were out of fear.

He crossed the room and claimed the chair across from her. "I don't think you wanted to perform plastic surgery on DiSanti, Dr. Manchester," he said quietly. "But I need you to tell me exactly what happened."

Emotions twisted her face, and she averted her gaze from his.

"If you're being coerced, I'll protect you."

She looked down at her hands, then lifted her head and her gaze met his. Emotions warred in her eyes. "Thank you, Mr. Hawk, but you can't help me. Mr. Polk is my attorney."

He studied her for a long minute, frustrated because he sensed she wanted his help, and that she needed it. But as Lucas said, their hands were tied.

He sighed, then stood. "All right. If you change your mind, let me know."

She stared at the card he laid on the table, but didn't pick it up. He waited another minute, hoping she'd change her mind, but she dropped her gaze to her hands again and remained silent.

Those hands had given DiSanti a new face so he could escape and continue spearheading the Shetland operation.

The man was despicable and needed to be put away.

If he was wrong about Dr. Manchester, she deserved to be prosecuted, as well.

Still, his gut churned as he left the room.

Chapter Five

Frustration filled Brayden as he watched Lucas lock Mila Manchester in a holding cell.

He thought she was terrified and had been coerced. But what if her teary eyes and trembling hands were part of a well-orchestrated act?

Lessons learned in the past taunted him.

He'd been fooled once by a client's lies. A pretty young woman who'd batted innocent-looking eyes at him and cried on his shoulder. A woman who'd used him to put her boyfriend away for a crime that she'd committed. He'd gotten her off, then realized that she was a manipulative user.

Thankfully, she'd tried her scam on another guy and been caught red-handed.

But he'd walked away feeling like a fool and had vowed never to fall for another pretty face again.

Still, the sight of the doctor's forlorn expression as she sank onto that dingy narrow cot made his gut tighten.

He turned away and noticed the same frustration in Lucas's scowl.

"Charlotte's going to be angry," Lucas said between gritted teeth.

Sympathy for Lucas swelled inside him. Charlotte had gone through hell because of the Shetland ring. She'd been injured, had lost her vision for some time and had been sick with worry about her students who'd been kidnapped. She had good reason to want DiSanti locked away.

The fact that she praised the doctor's humanitarianism spoke volumes on Dr. Manchester's behalf.

"What are you going to do?" he asked Lucas.

"Check out that lawyer," Lucas said. "Maybe we can find something to charge him with and force Dr. Manchester's hand."

"I could talk to her coworkers," Brayden offered.

Lucas shrugged. "You aren't her lawyer, Brayden."

Brayden walked beside Lucas until they reached the front door of the field office. "I know. But I might find out something to explain why Dr. Manchester performed surgery on that monster. It just doesn't feel right."

Lucas nodded. "I agree. I'll get our analyst to pull up everything she can find on Polk as well as the doctor."

"There has to be something DiSanti's people used to force her to work for them," Brayden said. "Maybe an indiscretion in the past."

"Or maybe she met him when she was volunteering abroad," Lucas suggested. "Seeing the vast needs and poverty in the underprivileged areas she visited may have driven her to accept money to fund her clinic."

True. For Charlotte's sake, he hoped not.

"You want me to drive Charlotte home?" Brayden asked.

Lucas shook his head. "I need to talk to her myself."

He didn't envy that conversation between his brother and Charlotte.

Meanwhile, he'd talk to Dexter. His PI skills could be helpful in finding information on the doctor's clinic and her coworkers.

Talking to them might provide insight into what had driven Mila Manchester to break the law.

MILA DROPPED HER face into her hands, her body shaking with worry and fear. Where was Izzy now?

Was she safe? Was the nanny still with her? Or had the men taken Izzy somewhere else so the police couldn't find her in case a neighbor reported a disturbance at the house?

She rose and paced the cell, her agitation mounting. The image of that man holding a gun to Roberta and Izzy taunted her. Izzy must be terrified.

She was only three. A tiny little pip-squeak of a girl with big dark eyes and an infectious laugh and an obsession with playing dress up. She loved dolls and pretending she was a princess with a tiara and poufy skirt.

But other times she liked to dig in the earth and play with worms and kick the soccer ball in the backyard.

Izzy had started a campaign to convince Santa to bring her a puppy for Christmas and had drawn pictures and cards of how she'd take care of the animal.

She liked strawberry ice cream with sprinkles and brownies and loved mac and cheese. She enjoyed making her own pizza and PB&J sandwiches. She snacked on carrots and cheese, and apples with peanut butter and wanted b-b's, blueberries, for breakfast with her pancakes.

She hated tuna fish, turned her nose up at broccoli and stirred her green peas around on the plate to make it look like she'd eaten some when she hadn't put a single pea in her mouth.

She was stubborn and loud and messy and got up way too early on the weekends, but Mila loved her with all her heart.

Another wave of fear washed over her.

Even if she did exactly what DiSanti's men instructed her to do, how could she trust that they'd let her go and release Izzy and Roberta?

What if she did everything they demanded, but they killed her when they were finished?

What would happen to her daughter?

She heaved a breath, her lungs aching for air as panic seized her.

Would DiSanti keep her hostage or sell her into his sex slavery business when Izzy got older?

The thought made her so sick inside that she sank onto that thin mattress, then dropped her head down between her knees to keep from passing out.

BRAYDEN TRIED TO stay out of the way as Lucas explained the situation to his wife.

Charlotte burst into tears. "You can't do this, Lucas," Charlotte cried.

Lucas rubbed his wife's arms. "Brayden offered to represent her, but this other lawyer showed up, and she deferred to him."

"There has to be an explanation," Charlotte said.

"If there is, we'll get to the bottom of it." Lucas wrapped his arms around Charlotte and hugged her, the bond between them so strong it made Brayden envious. When they pulled apart, he stroked her arms. "I'll check out this lawyer tonight and see what I can find on him."

He glanced at Brayden as if he needed backup, and Brayden fought a chuckle. Nothing scared Lucas more than failing his wife.

"Hang in there, Charlotte. I'm going to look into Dr. Manchester's coworkers and see if they know what's going on," Brayden said.

She still looked worried, but she nodded and thanked him.

Brayden said good-night to them then hurried out to his SUV. As soon as he got inside, he phoned Dexter and explained the situation.

"I'll see what I can dig up on her and her staff," Dexter said.

"Let's examine her financials," Brayden said. "If DiSanti paid her, the money should show up somewhere."

"I'm on it," Dexter agreed.

"We need all the information we can gather before Dr. Manchester bonds out," Brayden said. "DiSanti has long-reaching tentacles across the world. If Polk takes her out of the country, we may never see her again."

MILA FINALLY LAY back on the cot. She doubted she could sleep, but she was so exhausted from the grueling hours of surgery and from worrying about her daughter that she practically collapsed.

She closed her eyes and said a prayer that Izzy and Roberta were all right. Roberta loved Izzy and would protect her if she could.

The fact that she might not be able to frightened her the most.

Polk said Izzy was all right. For now.

She had to do whatever they said. She'd give her life to save Izzy.

Carina's young face flashed in her mind. Izzy looked a little like Carina. She just hoped DiSanti didn't see himself in Izzy's eyes.

She hadn't heard from Carina since the night she'd fled in terror. Not that she expected to. But she couldn't help but wonder if the girl was still in school, if she'd found friends or a family where she fit in.

She'd suffered so much abuse at such a young age. That kind of trauma affected most people for life. Add to that trauma the fact that she'd given birth to a baby alone, a baby born from a rape. And then she'd given that child away.

A certain amount of guilt might plague her for that decision, although she had no reason to feel guilty. She'd made the most unselfish choice she could make—she'd put her baby's future before her own.

Had Carina been able to overcome the emotional trauma and focus on making a future for herself?

Unable to keep her eyes open any longer, she finally

fell into a deep sleep, a sleep filled with nightmares that made her wrestle with the hard pillow on the cot.

She and Izzy were at the beach. The warm sunshine played off her daughter's dark hair as she raced along the edge of the water. Mila chased after her, laughing as Izzy darted back and forth to dodge the waves. She loved the water and the sand and the creatures they found on the beach.

They watched a baby crab disappear into his home underground, then used plastic sand toys to dig and create a castle complete with a moat. Izzy laughed as she spilled water from the bucket all over her feet, then squealed when Mila picked her up and swung her around.

She dropped her onto the middle of a whale-shaped float, and Izzy laughed in delight as she bounced on a wave.

The next minute, Izzy was screaming in terror. The sun and ocean had disappeared, and a big man was hauling her daughter from their house. Izzy kicked and cried, but the man clamped his hand over her mouth, then tossed her in the back of a van.

Tires squealed and the van screeched away.

A gunshot sounded and Roberta ran after the van. Then Roberta was gone, and the van lurched to a stop at a dark, rotting shed somewhere in the desert. It had to be a million degrees during the day.

And frigid at night.

Desperate to find her daughter, Mila combed the desert, walking miles and miles until she fell face-first into the scorching sand. A storm surfaced, and sand swirled and swirled around her in a blur. She couldn't see anything, not even her own hand in front of her.

Another scream. Izzy. She was lost out there in the sandstorm.

Izzy screamed again, and Mila pushed herself to her hands and knees and crawled forward.

What was that man doing to her daughter?

She had to get to her, to save her…

She was walking again, then running, her feet miring down into the sand…

Then Izzy was in front of her, her little body unmoving, the sand covering her as it raged through the air. She dug with her hands, determined to reach her, but the sand was burying her like quicksand…

Mila jerked awake, shaking and crying, her heart sinking as Izzy disappeared into the ground.

BRAYDEN LOVED THE RANCH, but he and his brothers needed privacy now they were older and busy. Still, his mother had kept rooms for them to use when they visited. Recently, Harrison and Lucas had both built houses on Hawk's Landing for them and their wives.

Brayden and Dex also had offices in Austin. Brayden had rented an apartment above his law office, and Dex found a cabin on the edge of town that he could work out of, as well.

Brayden drove to Dexter's, knowing he couldn't go home and sleep right away, not when Mila Manchester's sad eyes haunted him.

Dexter greeted him with a cold beer. His brother had a state-of-the-art computer system and was a whiz at finding information on the web. Sometimes he sensed

Dex didn't follow the rules; then again, that was the reason he'd formed his own PI agency instead of studying law.

If he crossed the line, Brayden didn't want to know about it. So far, Lucas and Harrison hadn't asked questions either. As sheriff, Harrison had called on Dex for help a few times. He was pretty sure Lucas had, too, but Lucas only shared information on a need-to-know basis.

Dex pressed a few keys and a photo of the doctor appeared along with articles on her services for the needy.

"Look at this," Dexter said. "Judging from the awards and press Mila's received, she's everything Charlotte claims. She practically runs her own clinic and offers services pro bono for families and children in need across the country. Hell, across the world."

Brayden's gaze skated over the dozens of articles featuring Mila's mother, Andrea Manchester, and had to agree.

"She's following in her mother's footsteps." Dexter accessed a photo of Mila's mother receiving an award for her Doctors Without Borders work, just a month before she died in a shooting in Syria. She'd operated on a child born with a cleft lip and cleft palate.

"I suppose it's possible Mila became overwhelmed with the vast needs for her services and the cost, and accepted money to fund her efforts," Dexter said. "But my preliminary search into her financials didn't reveal anything suspicious. No large deposits, no offshore accounts." He gestured toward another computer screen showing the doctor's personal account then her business one. "There is an account for donations that has around a hundred grand, but it'll take me time to sort through the ins and outs of the accounting to see if all the donations are legit."

Brayden scrubbed a hand through his hair. Money could be one motive. But if she'd been coerced, there had to be a more personal reason. "How about family? Does she have parents, a sister or brother, anyone DiSanti might threaten to persuade her to do his dirty work?"

"Wait, this is interesting," Dexter said.

Brayden shifted, hoping his brother had found something he could use to convince Mila to talk to him. "What?"

"Mila was adopted, although both of her adopted parents have passed," Dexter said.

Brayden's brows shot up. "Any information on her birth mother or father?"

Dexter shook his head. "Apparently she was abandoned as a baby. No father listed anywhere. Dr. Andrea Manchester was working at the hospital where Mila was brought in by paramedics. She and her husband adopted Mila."

No wonder she'd wanted to follow in her mother's footsteps. "Anything on her coworkers?" Brayden asked.

Dexter shrugged. "The head nurse is a single mother named Rhoda Zimmerman. She has a ten-year-old son and lives close to the clinic." He pressed the print button and the printer spit out a page of names and addresses. "Other employees include a receptionist, another nurse and a PA."

Brayden checked his watch. "It's too late tonight to

talk to any of them. But first thing in the morning, I'll get on it."

"It'll go faster if we divide the list," Dexter said.

"Thanks. I'll take the head nurse and receptionist."

"I'll talk to the others," Dexter offered.

Brayden noticed a file on the desk, one that was labeled Hawk. His gaze shot to his brother, then he gestured to the folder. "What's that about?"

A wary look flashed across Dexter's chiseled face. "A file on Chrissy."

"You were looking for her all these years?"

Dex nodded. "Glad that's settled."

Unfortunately, she was dead and had been since the day she'd gone missing.

"Guess I can put it away now." His brother swept the folder off the desk and jammed it in the drawer.

Something about how quickly he removed it made Brayden suspicious. He could usually read his brother like a book. But not tonight.

Was Dexter keeping something from him?

Chapter Six

Mila jerked awake from her nightmares, only to realize that she was living a real one. The dark holding cell was cold and lonely, and felt a million miles away from home and her daughter.

She scrubbed her hands over her eyes, wiping away more tears. If she lost Izzy, she didn't know what she'd do.

Desperate to keep it together until she was released so she could find her little girl, she forced her mind to her work.

Images of former patients, children in need, their parents' gratitude that she'd given their children a chance at a normal life, flashed behind her eyes.

Little Robin, who had a scar from falling through a window. Seven-year-old Jacob, who'd suffered abuse at his father's hands—she'd repaired the damage to his face, although the sweet child would never get his vision back in his left eye. Tiny Sariana, whose leg had been burned in a car accident. Baby Jane Doe, who'd been left for dead in the woods and mauled by an animal.

There were other children and families out there who needed her.

But what would they think if they discovered she'd given a new face to a human trafficker so he could escape?

Carina had borne the brunt of his vile ways and barely survived.

Mila had promised to protect her baby. But she'd failed. Now Izzy was in the hands of DiSanti's goons.

We know you helped some of our girls escape, the man who'd stormed into her clinic had said.

She massaged her temple. How had they known?

Had they been watching her? Or had they found one of the girls and forced her to talk? Maybe they'd discovered the underground ring that helped women and children and young girls escape abuse to find a better life?

Carina… Was she safe and still in hiding?

BRAYDEN WOKE TO a text from Lucas.

Bond hearing for Dr. Manchester at ten a.m.

Brayden took a quick shower, then dressed and rushed out the door. He drove to the diner near him, picked up coffee and a sausage biscuit and wolfed it down as he drove to Dr. Manchester's clinic.

It normally opened at eight. A truck and sedan sat in the parking lot while an SUV was parked in the employees' spaces. He spotted a woman in a nurse's uniform at the door with an older lady holding a baby, and a thirtyish woman with a teenage boy.

"I'm sorry, folks, the clinic is closed today," the nurse said. "Dr. Manchester won't be here."

Brayden hung back and listened to see if she offered more of an explanation, but she didn't.

"We'll reschedule as soon as I hear from her and we adjust our schedule," the nurse said.

The lady with the baby walked toward the sedan and the young woman and teenager climbed in the truck.

Brayden approached the nurse cautiously. If she conspired to help DiSanti, he'd find out.

The nurse tacked a sign saying Closed on the door, then retrieved keys from her purse.

"Excuse me, Miss Zimmerman?"

Her eyes widened as she looked up at him. "Yes?"

"The clinic is closed?"

"I'm afraid so. Did you have an appointment?"

He shook his head.

"Well, if you need one, call back and leave your number, and I'll have our receptionist get back to you."

"I'm not a patient," Brayden said, then introduced himself. "Were you aware that Dr. Manchester was operating on a wanted fugitive yesterday?"

The nurse gasped. "What? My God, that's not true."

"I'm afraid it is." He showed her a picture of DiSanti. "Do you recognize this man?"

The shock on her face looked real. "No, I've never seen him before. Why do you think he was here?"

"We know he was here," Brayden said matter-of-factly. "You didn't see him yesterday?"

She shook her head again. "No. And Dr. Manchester would never help a criminal, not if she knew who he was. She devotes her time to families, especially children in need."

That was what everyone kept saying. "Maybe so, but she performed plastic surgery on him yesterday."

A tense second passed. She shifted, then glanced through the glass door with a frown.

"What is it? You know something," Brayden said. "Were you working yesterday?"

She nodded, her eyes dark with emotions he couldn't quite define. "I did, but Dr. Manchester asked me to clear out the waiting room and sent me home early. She said her daughter was sick and she had to leave."

"Her daughter?" That was news. "I didn't realize she had a child."

The nurse's expression softened. "Her name is Izzy. Dr. Manchester loves that little girl like crazy."

"Did she seem upset? Afraid?"

Her brows furrowed. "Come to think of it, she did seem a little nervous. But I just thought she was worried about Izzy."

"Did you see anyone else here? Maybe a car in the parking lot?"

"I didn't really notice. There could have been, but I went out the front door." Worry deepened the grooves beside her eyes. "Why? What's going on?"

"That's what I'm trying to figure out," Brayden said. "Sometime after you left work yesterday, the FBI discovered that DiSanti and his crew were here and stormed the clinic. Dr. Manchester was arrested."

The nurse gasped. "My God, that's not right. Mila would never—"

"She did," Brayden said. "And I think she may have been threatened."

The woman clamped her lips together, then fumbled

with her keys. "I don't know what to tell you. But I'm going to stop by her house and check on Izzy and the nanny."

Brayden put his hand over hers. "No, I'll go by and check on them."

If something was wrong with Izzy and the nanny, it might be dangerous.

He thanked her, then phoned Dexter on his way to Dr. Manchester's home address and filled him in. "She has a daughter?" Dex asked.

"According to her head nurse, yes. Her name is Izzy."

"That's odd. There's no mention of them in anything I've found about her. Dr. Manchester must keep her personal life very private."

He supposed he could understand that. But usually when people kept secrets, it meant they were hiding something.

"How about the father?" Dex asked.

"No information on him." Brayden pulled a hand down his chin. "Is there any record that she was married?"

"I didn't see one," Dexter said.

So who was the little girl's father? "I'm driving by her house to check on the child and nanny, then to the field office for the bond hearing."

"I put calls in to the other staff. I'll let you know if they add anything to what you've already learned."

Brayden thanked him, then hung up and veered toward Dr. Manchester's. She lived in a small neighborhood outside Austin, only a few miles from her clinic. He searched the area as he drove down the street. Most of the houses were renovated ranches and bungalows.

Judging from the children's bikes and toys dotting the yards, the neighborhood catered to young families. The yards were well kept, complete with fall decorations and pumpkins.

Dr. Manchester lived in a Craftsman-style house at the end of the street. Her backyard jutted up to woods and land that hadn't yet been developed, offering privacy and a yard for her little girl to run and play.

Everything he'd learned indicated the plastic surgeon was the admirable selfless doctor that Charlotte, the nurse and the media claimed her to be.

But an uneasy feeling tightened his gut as he parked and walked up the drive. A dark green sedan sat in front of the garage, the only car on the premises. The nanny's? Two drives down, he noted a white van, and across the street, a black Cadillac. The neighbors'?

He scanned the front porch and windows, but the blinds were closed, and he couldn't see inside. Nothing outside looked amiss though. And he didn't hear signs that anyone was inside.

He punched the doorbell and tapped his foot as he waited. A minute later, he raised his fist and knocked. If he didn't get an answer, he was going to check around back, see if a window was open.

Footsteps shuffled inside. A low voice. Female?

He straightened and pasted on a smile as the door opened slightly. A short dark-haired woman peered up at him.

"My name is Brayden Hawk," he said. "I'm a friend of Dr. Manchester's. I stopped by the clinic to see her, but the clinic was closed today so I thought she might be home."

"I'm afraid not. I can tell her you stopped by." She started to close the door, but Brayden caught it with his hand.

He studied her, searching for signs she was upset or being coerced somehow. "The nurse said the doctor's daughter was sick. Is she here?"

The woman's eyes darted to the side, then she nodded. "In bed. She has a fever and needs rest."

He slipped his business card into her hand. "I hope it's nothing serious," he said. "If you need anything, call me."

The woman's hand trembled as she jammed the business card in her apron pocket. "I'm sorry, mister. I need to go take care of her." She didn't wait for a response. She closed the door in his face.

MILA CLASPED HER clammy hands together as she waited on the lawyer to meet her before the bond hearing. Nerves bunched in her stomach, and her head throbbed from lack of sleep.

The door to the interrogation room creaked open, and Agent Hawk appeared with Polk. His beady eyes skated over her, threatening and unrelenting.

"You have five minutes," Agent Hawk said as he glanced between the two of them. "Then it's time to see the judge."

"It will only take two," Polk said curtly.

Fluorescent light accentuated Polk's bald head. He strode toward her, then claimed the chair across from her, his lips set in a firm line.

"Is my daughter all right?" Mila asked in a low whisper.

His thick brows furrowed together into a unibrow.

"As I said last night, she will be fine as long as you do what you're told."

"Please let me go home to her," Mila said. "I promise not to tell anyone about yesterday. I've been here all night and I didn't say a word."

"*He* had a rough night," Polk said, as if he didn't intend to incriminate himself by saying DiSanti's name aloud. "Once he's on his way to recovery, you and your daughter will be reunited."

Would she?

"How do I know you're not lying, that you haven't killed her already?" Mila crossed her arms. "I want proof that she's safe, then I'll do whatever you ask."

Polk cursed, then pulled his phone from his pocket and accessed a photograph.

Tears choked Mila's throat. It was Izzy in her room. The princess clock on her nightstand read 7:00 a.m. Not long ago.

Izzy was curled in bed with her pink blanket and baby doll clutched to her. Relief made her shoulders sag.

But it was temporary.

DiSanti never left a witness behind. When he'd kidnapped Charlotte's students, his men had shot Charlotte and left her for dead. In fact, she was the only one who'd survived his men.

If they killed her when she finished nursing that monster DiSanti back to health, who would raise Izzy?

Chapter Seven

Brayden shared what he'd learned about Mila with Lucas as they entered the courtroom.

"I know you want her to be innocent and so does Charlotte," Lucas said. "And you may be right. But unless she speaks up, my hands are tied."

The court was called to order, and Lucas quieted as the judge heard two cases, then Mila's. It took no time for the judge to grant Mila's bond. Her lawyer kept a tight rein on her, his shoulder touching hers as they exited as if he needed to keep her close. Mila remained silent, her hands knotted, body tense.

Her gaze darted to him as they reached the exit, then Polk took her arm and ushered her outside.

He and Lucas followed. Brayden's instincts screamed that something was wrong. Maybe the nanny had lied to him. Maybe Izzy wasn't sick, but someone had been in that house holding a gun on her.

Or maybe his imagination was running wild. Maybe he was projecting what he wanted to be true onto Mila.

Just like he had that other woman. He'd long ago stopped using her name. It hurt too much to think what a fool he'd been.

He wouldn't repeat the same mistake.

Morning sunshine shimmered off the autumn leaves as they exited the courtroom and made their way to the steps of the courthouse. Traffic slogged by, pedestrians hurrying to breakfast and work, mingling with joggers and parents pushing baby strollers toward the park two blocks down.

Mila tucked her head down as they descended the steps. Polk kept a firm grip on Mila's arm as if he expected her to bolt any minute, then steered her to the right toward a parking deck.

"I don't like this," Brayden said.

"Neither do I." Lucas quickened his pace to keep Polk and Mila in sight, and Brayden kept up with him. Polk guided her across the busy street to the exit of the parking deck, one hand shoved in his jacket pocket.

"He's got a gun." Lucas darted across the street and Brayden sprinted after him, dodging a car that screeched to a stop barely an inch from him.

Brayden threw up a hand to apologize, but didn't have time to slow down. Mila's terrified gaze met his, making his heart skip a beat.

"Wait!" Lucas shouted as he jogged toward Polk.

A dark van pulled up beside Polk, and Polk reached for the door handle.

"Stop, Polk!" Lucas shouted again.

But the man spun around and fired at Lucas and then at Brayden. Brayden jumped to the side, and Lucas ducked behind the rear of the van for cover. People shouted and ran from the street into the parking deck, coffee shop and neighboring stores. Police officers raced from the courthouse outside to clear the streets and provide backup.

Lucas inched toward the side of the van and fired at Polk. He retaliated by opening fire and shoving Mila toward the van. She screamed, stumbling, then hit the ground on her hands and knees. A short robust beefy guy jumped out and grabbed Mila.

"Let her go!" Brayden yelled.

Lucas fired at Polk again, and this time Lucas's bullet hit home. The man's body bounced back as the bullet penetrated his chest, then he staggered and collapsed.

Brayden lunged toward Mila, but the gunman put his weapon to her head. Brayden froze, cold terror slamming into him.

Lucas took cover at the edge of the vehicle, his gaze meeting Brayden's. Brayden understood. He needed to create a distraction.

Brayden held up his hands in surrender mode. "You don't want to do this, buddy. Just release the doctor and no one else gets hurt."

The beefy guy shook his head and pushed Mila toward the van. She cried out and slammed into the side of it.

Lucas inched up behind the bastard and jammed his gun in the man's back. "Drop it. Now."

The bastard spun around and swung the butt of his gun toward Lucas's head. Lucas knocked it away and they fought, then Lucas sent the man's gun sailing to the ground.

Mila darted away from the gunman and hit the ground a few feet away.

The brute lurched for his weapon, but Lucas fired,

hitting the man in the chest. Blood spattered, and Lucas ran to him, then kicked the man's gun into the shrubs.

Brayden rushed forward and helped Mila to stand. She was shaken and in shock, her body trembling as she collapsed against him.

Shouts erupted, and several officers jogged toward them to assist. Lucas gestured for Brayden to get Mila inside. He wrapped his arm around her waist and coaxed her back into the building in case more of DiSanti's men were watching.

An officer rushed toward Brayden as they stood in the corner in the lobby of the courthouse. "Anyone hurt? Do you need medical assistance?"

Brayden tilted Mila's face up so he could examine her for injuries, then checked her clothes for blood. "Are you hurt, Mila?"

She shook her head, but terror glazed her eyes.

He pulled her to him and rubbed her back to calm her. "Can you take us to a room where we can wait on Agent Hawk?"

"Of course." The officer led the way down a hall then into a conference room. "I'll get some water."

Brayden nodded and ushered Mila toward one of the sofas. Instead of sitting down though, she grabbed his shirt lapel. "You shouldn't have stopped him! You should have let me go!" Tears rained down her face as she pummeled him with her fists. "Why didn't you just let me handle the situation!"

"Because you were in trouble."

"I had it under control," Mila cried.

Brayden swallowed hard, then forced a calm voice.

"Lucas saw Polk's gun. He thought he was going to hurt you."

"You don't know what you've done! You…you should have let me go." Sobs racked her body, and he grabbed her fists in his hands and held them to his chest.

"I know you're upset, but Polk was dangerous and so was the bastard who shot at us."

She gave up the fight and sagged against him. He held her and stroked her back to calm her, murmuring low, soothing words. "It's going to be all right, Mila. I promise."

She pushed back, anger slashing her eyes as she swiped at her tears. "No, it's not. You don't know what you're talking about."

"Then tell me what's going on," he said. "Why you helped DiSanti. Why you were willing to go with a man who had a gun on you and probably planned to kill you when he got you away from here."

A helpless look passed through her eyes, followed by fear and panic. She choked on another cry, then dropped her head into her hands. Her body shook again, more tears falling.

His mind raced with possible scenarios, all of which he didn't like. All of which involved her safety or the safety of her nanny and little girl.

He gave her a few minutes, took the water from the officer who entered with it, then slipped the bottle into her hand.

"Drink."

She twisted the cap, but her hand shook so badly that she dropped it onto the floor. She guzzled half the bottle before setting it on the coffee table in front of her.

When she looked at him, despair seemed to weigh her down.

He retrieved the bottle cap and set it on the table. "Mila, I know that you're a good person. Charlotte vouched for you. I saw your awards, and talked to your head nurse. I also know you have a daughter."

Her lower lip quivered.

"If you tell me the truth, I promise I'll help you."

Her face crumpled. "They have her," she said in a haunted whisper. "They threatened her if I didn't cooperate." Anger hardened her voice. "Do you know what that means?"

Her tormented gaze met his, his heart pounding.

"It means you and your brother may have just gotten my little girl killed."

MILA BIT HER tongue to keep from confiding the rest of the story to Brayden. But she'd sworn not to reveal the truth about Izzy's mother or father to anyone, and she had to keep that promise.

It was the only way to keep her daughter safe.

Her heart pounded. She shouldn't have told him anything.

But what choice did she have?

"Let me get Lucas. He can help—"

"No." Mila grabbed his hand. "You said whatever I told you was in confidence."

Brayden shifted, his eyes assessing her. "If you want me as your lawyer, yes, everything you tell me is private."

She released a sigh of relief. "Agent Hawk is your brother though—"

"It doesn't matter," Brayden said. "We're both professionals. He knew when he allowed me to talk to you that I was bound by attorney-client privilege."

Mila wanted to believe him. She had to trust someone. And he seemed sincere.

Brayden made a low sound in his throat. "I'm sorry, Mila. I can call you that, can't I?"

"I don't care what you call me," Mila said. "All I want is to protect my daughter."

Brayden nodded. "Yesterday when I talked to you, I suspected something was off, so I did some digging. You didn't ask to call anyone when Lucas brought you in, which was odd. When I learned about your daughter, I put two and two together. I went by this morning to check out the situation."

Mila's eyes widened. "You saw Izzy? Was she okay?"

Brayden hesitated, agitating her more. "Your nanny answered the door. She said Izzy was in bed, that she was sick."

Mila's pulse clamored. "But you didn't see her?"

He shook his head. "I'm afraid not."

Panic shot through her, and she dug her fingers into his arm. "I have to go to her, see her myself. Get her somewhere safe. Once DiSanti realizes what happened here today, he may hurt her or take her away somewhere."

Brayden nodded. "I'll tell Lucas where we're going."

"No," Mila cried. "Don't you understand? He has men at my house. They have guns. Izzy and I were FaceTiming when they burst in and took them hostage."

Brayden laid his hand over Mila's. The human contact felt comforting and made her want to spill everything to him.

But she still had secrets.

Secrets she had to keep to protect her daughter.

BRAYDEN STUDIED MILA AGAIN, grateful she'd finally come clean. Lucas wouldn't like being left in the dark, but Brayden was bound by confidentiality, and he would honor it.

Although it wouldn't take Lucas long to figure out what was going on himself.

He'd researched the lawyer. No doubt the FBI already knew about Mila's daughter.

"Please," Mila said. "I need to see Izzy."

He nodded. "You said men with guns were at the house. It's too dangerous."

Mila shot up. "I don't care. She's my little girl, and she needs me. Now either take me to her or let me go."

"We'll talk to my brother. He can send the FBI there to rescue her," Brayden said.

She shook her head no. "They will kill her if they see the feds or cops."

He touched her arm again. The simple contact sent a tingle of awareness through him that he had no business feeling for a client, much less a woman in trouble with both the law and a man liked DiSanti.

But being with her was the only way to keep her from getting hurt and to learn the truth—if she was lying about her part in DiSanti's surgery.

"I'll drive you, but you have to do as I say and stay in the car."

Her gaze locked with his for a brief moment. Finally she gave a nod.

"I'll tell Lucas that you're upset, that I'm taking you someplace so we can talk."

Indecision warred in her eyes. "That's *all* you'll tell him."

He nodded. "Trust me, Mila."

But the odd flicker in her eyes indicated she didn't trust anyone. He wondered who'd betrayed her to the point that she felt that way.

None of your business. A little girl's life might be at stake.

He had to do his job.

Then again, she might be right not to trust. DiSanti had people everywhere. For all he knew, the man might own a judge or a cop or even a fed…

He stepped to the door to text Lucas. His brother was in the hall, so he joined him.

"How is she?" Lucas asked.

"Shaken, but physically all right."

"We need to convince her to tell us more about Di-Santi."

"I'm aware of that." Brayden held up a hand. "But she's scared, Lucas."

Lucas studied him for a minute, obviously torn. "You think she was coerced, don't you?"

Brayden pasted on his poker face but gave a slight nod. "Release her into my custody, Lucas. I'll get to the bottom of this. I promise."

Lucas studied him for a long moment. "All right. But don't let her get away. She's the only lead we have to DiSanti."

He knew that. But he was more worried about her child at the moment than catching that monster.

"I'll have an officer escort you to your SUV just in case DiSanti's men are watching."

He thanked his brother, then ducked back into the room and told Mila he'd cleared her to leave with him. When they exited the room, the officer was waiting.

Brayden took Mila's arm, and the guard led them from the building to his SUV.

"I've got it from here." Brayden dismissed the guard, and the officer turned and walked back to the courthouse.

"I'm going to call my brother Dexter to meet us at the house. He's a PI."

"You promised that everything I told you was confidential," Mila said sharply.

He angled himself toward her. "It is. But I'm not a fool either, Mila. These men are dangerous. We'd be crazy to go there without backup."

"But he might call Lucas—"

Brayden shook his head. "Dex likes to bend the rules. We've kept more than one secret from Lucas and Harrison, our other brother who's sheriff of Tumbleweed." He paused, teeth gritted. "If there's anyone I trust to keep your secret, it's Dex."

A world of doubt settled in her eyes, but she must have realized that she didn't have much choice and agreed. He phoned Dexter, gave him a brief rundown and asked him to meet them at Mila's.

When he hung up, he started the engine and pulled into traffic. A strained silence stretched between him and Mila as he drove.

When he neared her house, he slowed and waited five doors down until Dex arrived. Dex climbed in the back seat and he made quick introductions, then coasted past Mila's to survey the house and property.

Everything looked quiet.

Mila leaned forward, searching, worry creating lines around her mouth and eyes.

He turned around at the end of the street, then drove two houses away and parked on the street. "Stay here, Mila. Dex and I will find Izzy."

She clenched her hands in terror, but gave a small nod. Dammit, he hated to leave her in the car. What if DiSanti's men were watching and grabbed her from his SUV?

"You can stay with her," Dex said as if he read Brayden's mind.

"No," Mila said. "I'll be fine. It'll take both of you to handle the men."

"She's right," Brayden said. "If you can stave off the goons, I'll get Izzy and the nanny outside."

He gave Mila's hand a quick squeeze, retrieved his gun from the dash, then he and Dexter slipped from the car. They ducked through the neighbor's backyard, staying low in the bushes as they approached the back deck of Mila's house.

He just prayed the nanny and Izzy were still here, and that he and Dexter could get them out alive.

Chapter Eight

Brayden gestured for Dexter to check the door while he crept up to the back window and peered inside.

The interior was dark and quiet. He didn't see movement, but the hallway offered no view of the interior of the rooms.

He mouthed to Dex that he didn't see anyone, then kept watch while his brother climbed the steps to the deck and inched to the door. His brother held his gun at the ready and checked the doorknob.

The door screeched open.

Not a good sign.

Dex gave him a questioning look, and Brayden joined him, careful not to make a sound.

Senses alert, Brayden peered inside the doorway.

No movement. Except for the low hum of the furnace, no sound came from the house.

Odd.

The hair on the back of Brayden's neck prickled. This morning the nanny had been here.

Now the place felt eerily empty.

Did DiSanti's men know about the shooting at the courthouse? Had they left with Mila's daughter?

That wouldn't be good…

Dexter headed down the hall, and Brayden followed close behind. They passed a powder room, which was empty, then two bedrooms, one on the left, the other on the right.

Brayden eased into the one on the right. Mila's. A white iron bed covered in a blue quilt, dresser on one wall, a walk-in closet and bath.

Dex checked the second room, then shook his head indicating no one was there.

Antsy now, Brayden pushed a third bedroom door open. Dex stood behind him, gun aimed in case an ambush awaited.

A white four-poster twin bed was covered in a pink comforter with dozens of dolls and stuffed animals scattered on top of it. A dollhouse occupied one corner. Blocks, puzzles and a pink baseball glove filled bookshelves in the corner. A pink sneaker lay on the floor by the dollhouse, missing its mate, and a board game looked as if someone had stepped on it. Maybe one of the goons?

The bed was unmade, closet empty. The space beneath the bed held a box of clothing and several mismatched socks.

No little girl here.

His gut tightened, and he gestured to Dexter that they should check the living room. Although at this point, it appeared no one was here.

Dex led the way with his gun still drawn. An acrid odor hit Brayden as they neared the front of the house.

The kitchen-living room was to the right, dining area on the left. A lamp had been overturned, magazines strewn on the floor, a muddy boot print left on the entrance by the door.

No sign of the nanny or Mila's little girl.

An open carton of milk sat on the kitchen counter along with boxes of crackers and snacks. The farmhouse table held a pizza box along with an empty Scotch bottle that he had a feeling didn't belong to Mila.

Dexter crossed to the table in search of something that might indicate where the men would have taken the nanny and Izzy.

The rancid odor hit Brayden again, and Brayden's stomach jolted as he spotted drops of blood spatter on the floor in the kitchen.

Nerves raw, he eased toward it, then peered around the edge of the counter, praying that Izzy wasn't there.

And that the blood didn't belong to her.

MILA WAS BARELY holding on by a thread.

She stared at the clock on the dashboard, counting the minutes and seconds as Brayden and his brother Dexter went inside her house. If they could just find Izzy and get her away from DiSanti's men, she would tell the Hawks everything.

Her mind turned to the Hawk men. Brayden looked to be in his early thirties, was tall and broad shouldered with dark, neatly trimmed hair. He was handsome and imposing in his suit like the lawyer he purported to be. But those boots hinted at a tough cowboy beneath. And so did those intense eyes.

How many Hawk men were there? Were they all in law enforcement?

What did it matter? As long as he saved her little

girl. Then she could worry about the charges against her. She hoped, if she gave the police a description of DiSanti, maybe worked with a sketch artist to convey an image of his new features, they'd drop the charges. She had been forced to perform surgery at gunpoint, her family threatened.

She twisted sideways and scanned the street. She'd bought this house because it was in a safe neighborhood. Because other families and children lived and played here. Because it was close to her work, and she could run home for lunch. Sometimes Roberta strolled Izzy up to the clinic when it was sunny, and they had a picnic in the park across the street.

The streets were empty now. Kids at school. Parents at work. Except for the mother of twins in the first house on the block. She'd seen the four-year-old little boys playing on the swing set in the backyard and kicking a ball around.

Mila raked a hand through her tangled hair, well aware she needed a shower and some clean clothes. She reeked of sweat and blood from the grueling hours on her feet the day before.

When this was over, maybe she should take some time off. Stay at home with Izzy for a while.

Sometimes she missed dinner and got home too late to put Izzy to bed. Moments like giggling at the table and reading bedtime stories meant everything to her now, even more than her work, which had driven her for as long as she could remember.

Although she'd wanted to be a role model for Izzy the way her adopted mother had been for her. Her adopted parents had taken Mila in when she was just a new-born, because her birth mother had abandoned her in a junkyard. A body shop repair mechanic searching for a fender to replace the one he'd torn off when he'd crashed into a tree had found her in a beat-up old Chevy.

If he hadn't been looking for that fender that day, she might not have survived.

She'd wanted to give Izzy the same chance at life that her adopted mother had given her.

She closed her eyes, bowed her head and prayed that she got the chance.

BLOOD SPATTERED THE FLOOR, cabinets and wall of the kitchen.

Brayden cursed, although relief mixed with anger. Not Izzy, thank God. But the nanny was dead.

She lay on her back, one arm above her head, the other on her chest, fingers curled toward her palms. She'd probably thrown her hands up to protect her face.

It hadn't done any good. The bullet pierced her forehead between her eyes. Blood dotted her forehead and cheeks and pooled beneath her head.

A professional hit.

Of course it would be. DiSanti's goons had no qualms about killing a woman. Rape and trafficking, selling young girls into sex slavery, was just a business to them. Bastards.

"No one's here," Dexter called from the living room.

Brayden motioned for him to come over. "They killed the nanny," Brayden said. "Gunshot to the head."

"Damn." Dexter appeared behind him, but both held back. The last thing they wanted was to contaminate the crime scene.

"It's my fault," Brayden said. "My visit this morning probably spooked them. So they killed her and took off with Izzy."

"Don't blame yourself. They probably got word of what happened at the courthouse," Dex said.

Brayden's lungs squeezed for air. "Mila warned me that if I interfered, I'd get her daughter killed."

Dex laid a hand on Brayden's back. "Stop. Izzy may still be all right. We'll find her."

But would they find her in time?

They needed a description of DiSanti's new face. But he understood Mila's reluctance. She was terrified and had a right to be. DiSanti was ruthless.

Other than the people who worked for him, Mila was the only person in the world who would recognize him now.

Which meant he would come after her. And he'd kill her so she wouldn't identify him.

"Call Lucas and get a crime scene unit out here," Brayden said. "I'm going to check on Mila."

He hurried to the door, then jogged outside toward his SUV.

MILA STARTLED WHEN Brayden knocked on the window. His grim expression as he unlocked the door and slid into the driver's seat made her stomach knot.

"What? Oh God, not Izzy—"

"No, Izzy wasn't there."

She bit back a cry, but was afraid to ask more.

"They must have taken off with her," he said softly.

"She's the only leverage they have to keep you quiet, and they know it, Mila."

Mila nodded, grasping onto hope that his logic was right.

Brayden cleared his throat. "I'm sorry to have to tell you this, Mila. But they killed your nanny."

She shook her head in denial. Roberta was gone.

Poor, sweet Roberta. Izzy loved her like a second mother. She'd met the woman at a shelter because she was homeless. Twenty years in an abusive relationship had taken its toll. Her husband, the man who'd beaten her too many times to count, had been shot by a gang member. His death meant her escape, except that she'd been destitute and determined not to fall into the trap of working for drug runners.

Mila had wanted to help her. It had been a blessing for all of them that Roberta had agreed to be a live-in nanny.

Now, because of her, Roberta was dead.

"Listen to me, Mila." Brayden gripped her arms and shook her gently to make her look at him. "I can see the wheels turning in your head. This was not your fault."

Mila fought tears, but they trickled down her cheeks anyway. "She wouldn't have been killed if she hadn't been working for me."

"Where would she have been, Mila?"

She jerked her gaze to his.

"I don't know much about her, but you obviously cared about her," Brayden said softly. "Did she have any other family?"

She shook her head. "No, her husband died because of gang activity. She was homeless and alone…"

"And you took her in and gave her a family," Brayden said, his voice tender.

She nodded. "She loved Izzy so much, and Izzy adored her."

Brayden cupped her face between his hands. "She knew that you loved her, and she died protecting the little girl she loved."

Mila clutched his arms, her heart aching. "Izzy must be so devastated. What if she witnessed them kill Roberta? She'll be traumatized and—"

"Shh," Brayden said softly. "One step at a time, Doc. I understand you're upset about your nanny, but right now we have to focus on finding Izzy."

He was right. But once she got Izzy back, she'd give Roberta the memorial service she deserved. She'd died protecting Izzy—she was a true hero.

"Focus on the fact that Izzy is all right. And remember, for now DiSanti needs you. He won't hurt Izzy, because he needs her as leverage."

"You can't tell your brother about what happened here," Mila insisted. "It's too dangerous for Izzy."

Brayden's expression looked torn. "I'm sorry, Mila. But there was a murder at your house. We have to report it. We can't leave Roberta lying there in the house for days."

Mila struggled with right and wrong, with grief and anger, with fear that no matter what she did, she might never see her little girl again.

"You can trust Lucas," Brayden said. "He may be a

federal agent, but he's a good guy. He'll protect Izzy and you."

It was still dangerous. And there was no way she could confide the truth about Izzy's father. No one could know.

"Mila?"

She clutched his arms, her mind racing. "Then you have to make sure that DiSanti knows that I haven't talked."

"We will," Brayden said. "I'll arrange for Lucas to make a statement to the press that you aren't cooperating with the FBI. All right?"

She bit her lower lip, but agreed. "What can we do to get my daughter back?"

Brayden stroked her arms. "First a crime team will process your house for forensics. Maybe the men who killed Roberta and took Izzy left evidence behind."

"Does it matter who they are?" Mila asked. "We know they work for that monster DiSanti."

"Identifying any one member of his group might lead us to some clue about DiSanti's plans or location. Lucas's people are analyzing Polk's and the gunman's phones, contact information and correspondence for any clue as to where DiSanti is hiding."

Mila's stomach churned, but she lifted her chin defiantly. "We have to do more. Give him some way to contact me." She'd even use herself as a pawn if she had to.

Chapter Nine

Emotions warred inside Brayden. It was beyond reprehensible that DiSanti would hurt a little girl.

Then again, they knew for a fact that he had hurt countless women and young girls, some as young as age twelve. To DiSanti and his people, the female population was put on earth to exploit. He did that for money without batting an eye.

Brayden couldn't help but wonder what had made the man so cold. Maybe his upbringing?

Not that it mattered. There was no excuse or justification.

He wanted the bastard to pay now more than ever.

But first, they had to get Izzy back safely.

Mila still looked uncertain about the plan. But what else could they do?

If he didn't work with Lucas, Dexter could try to track down DiSanti. But the FBI had resources that Dexter didn't.

Brayden believed in the law. But he wasn't stupid either. He'd learned to shoot a rifle when he was a teenager. His experience on the force had taught him how to handle a weapon, about apprehending a suspect, about when to shoot and not shoot.

Most of all, it had taught him that nothing could combat a bullet except one in return. Not a pretty lesson, but being street-smart meant surviving.

He didn't intend to die at the hands of DiSanti and allow him to continue his reign of terror.

"I need my cell phone," Mila said. "DiSanti's people might contact me through it."

"Good point."

"I probably should go back to the clinic," Mila suggested. "They might show up there."

"I don't think so. They know we'll be watching it," Brayden said.

The sound of an engine made them both jerk their heads around. Lucas.

Mila twisted her hands in her lap, fear returning to her eyes. "What if I'm doing the wrong thing? What if calling your brother gets Izzy killed?"

Brayden frowned, his pulse hammering. "Mila, I think we both know that you're in over your head. There's no way DiSanti will let you live, not when you're the only person outside his people who can identify him."

Her face turned ashen, but she didn't argue.

MILA RECOGNIZED THE truth in Brayden's words. But she didn't like it, and it scared the hell out of her to involve the FBI.

If they discovered Izzy wasn't her biological child and that DiSanti was Izzy's father, she might lose Izzy to him because of legality issues.

She'd have to watch every word she said to Brayden's brother. Only tell him what was necessary to find her daughter.

Agent Hawk slowed as he approached them, then pulled over and parked behind Brayden. Brayden climbed out to talk to his brother, and she studied the two, praying she hadn't made a mistake in trusting Brayden.

But Charlotte had married Lucas, so he must be an okay guy. When she'd first seen the news story on the shooting that had rendered Charlotte temporarily blind, she'd wanted to reach out to Charlotte, but she'd held back because of Izzy. She'd hated DiSanti and hoped the feds would find him and put him away for life.

She'd never imagined that she'd be the one to help him escape.

For a moment, Lucas and Brayden appeared to be in a heated argument. Brayden gestured toward her and her house. Finally, they both walked back to the car, and Brayden opened the passenger door.

"Lucas insists on speaking to you, Mila."

Her heart pounded, but she inhaled a deep breath. She'd do anything to protect her little girl, even lie to the FBI.

She slowly climbed from the vehicle, desperately wishing she'd had a shower. Maybe once they processed her house, they'd let her inside to gather some clothes.

"Dr. Manchester, Brayden explained the situation. I'm sorry that your nanny was killed. And most of all, sorry that your daughter is missing." His gaze seemed to be scrutinizing her as he spoke.

Mila cleared her throat. "He'll kill her if he thinks I talked to you."

Lucas nodded. "I understand your fear. And I promise that I'll do everything I can to bring your daughter home."

"Then you have to let him know that I haven't told you anything." She lifted her chin. "If it means locking me back up, then do it."

BRAYDEN GLANCED AT LUCAS, ready to argue if his brother agreed to put Mila back in a cell. She didn't belong there, not after all she'd suffered in the last twenty-four hours.

But a mother's love was so strong that he realized she'd do anything for her child, just as his mother would do anything for him and his brothers. She'd been devastated when their little sister had gone missing. They all had.

He'd blamed himself. So had his brothers.

And their father had just skipped out.

"I don't think that'll be necessary," Lucas said to Mila. "In fact, if DiSanti sent Polk after you, he'll send someone else."

Mila shivered. And this time she might not survive.

"I want to place you in protective custody until we catch DiSanti." Lucas speared Brayden with a questioning look. "Agreed?"

Brayden nodded. "I could drive her back to the ranch."

Mila twisted her hands together. "How will DiSanti contact me about Izzy?"

"She needs her phone," Brayden told Lucas.

Lucas nodded. "I can arrange that. Meanwhile, I'd like for you to work with a sketch artist."

Mila clamped her teeth over her bottom lip. "If you air a picture of his new face on the news, he'll know I talked."

"We won't release it to the public," Lucas said.

Mila folded her arms across her chest. "But what if someone in the police department or the FBI is working with DiSanti?"

Silence stretched between them, fraught with tension.

"She's right," Brayden said. "DiSanti may have people in his pocket that we don't know about."

Frustration darkened Lucas's eyes. "I promise you that I'll be discreet. I'll only share with people I trust. Once you make contact, and we get your daughter back, we'll go wide and launch a full-fledged hunt for the bastard."

A white crime scene van rolled up and slowed as it passed them.

"I need to meet them at the house," Lucas said.

Mila heaved a wary breath. "Would it be possible for me to go inside and get some clothes?"

Lucas and Brayden exchanged a look. "You don't need to see your nanny like she is now," Brayden said softly. "I can collect some things from inside for you if you want."

Lucas shrugged. "That would work. Give us time to process the house first." He narrowed his eyes at Brayden. "You didn't touch anything inside, did you?"

Brayden shook his head no. "Dex and I just searched the house. We found the nanny in the kitchen."

Mila clenched her hands together as if struggling to maintain control.

"I'll let you know when you can come in," Lucas said.

Lucas got back in his car and drove two houses down to Mila's.

Despair and worry knitted Mila's brow, making Brayden want to pull her into his arms and comfort her. To assure her that everything would be all right.

But he couldn't do that. Not when he had no idea where DiSanti's men had taken Izzy.

MILA WATCHED LUCAS and the crime team park in her driveway with a sense of trepidation.

That little bungalow was her home. She'd bought it with high hopes of settling there forever and giving Izzy a happy childhood full of sweet memories.

But Roberta was dead inside. And her daughter was a victim of a kidnapping...

Worse, Izzy might have witnessed her nanny's murder. Mila hoped not. But still, the trauma of those men holding her and Roberta at gunpoint could damage Izzy for a long time.

The images from that FaceTime call haunted her and always would. She could see the men bursting through the door. The guns aimed at Roberta and Izzy. Izzy screaming as that brute snatched her.

Once she got Izzy back, could they return to the house they'd once called home?

She didn't know...

"Mila, I realize this is a terrifying situation, but try to stay positive. DiSanti wants you, not Izzy."

Her breath grew painful in her chest. If DiSanti knew Izzy was his daughter, he would want Izzy.

And he'd kill Mila for keeping Izzy from him for the past three years. But Izzy would never have a normal life if DiSanti discovered the connection between them.

He'd probably hunt down Carina like a dog, too. Mila couldn't allow that to happen.

"I promise to do whatever is necessary to help apprehend him once we save Izzy," Mila said.

A long silence stretched between them as they both watched her house. Another van passed them and pulled into her drive.

"Who is that?" Mila asked.

"The ME. They'll transport Roberta's body to the morgue for an autopsy."

Her heart squeezed. The world had been a better place with Roberta's warm smile and love of life. Even if she and Izzy survived this, they would forever have a hole in their hearts where Roberta belonged.

"A crime scene crew can clean up after the investigators are finished," Brayden said.

"That would be nice." She was accustomed to the sight of blood from performing surgeries. But seeing Roberta's spilled from being murdered was different. Personal.

Brayden turned to face her. "Mila, I have to ask you something else."

She tensed at the grave sound of his voice.

"It's personal, but the reason I'm asking is that it might have some bearing on finding your daughter."

She inhaled a deep breath. "All right."

His blue eyes softened. "Is Izzy's father in her life?"

Oh God... She forced herself to remain calm. "Why do you want to know about him?"

He shrugged. "We know DiSanti orchestrated this situation, but should we contact Izzy's father?"

"He's not in her life and never has been." At least that was true.

Another pause. "Is it possible then that he might have taken a payoff to help DiSanti get to you?"

Mila understood his question now. Oftentimes in kidnappings, a parent was involved.

That was certainly true in her case. But not for the reasons that Brayden thought.

She faced him with an earnest expression, hoping to end this line of questioning once and for all.

"That's not possible. Izzy's father is dead," Mila said.

Chapter Ten

Mila was so antsy she thought she would come out of her skin as she waited on the crime scene team to finish with her house.

All she could think about was where they'd taken Izzy. What was happening to her? Was she hurt?

Izzy didn't like scary movies or TV shows. Izzy insisted Mila and Roberta check the closets and under the beds for monsters at bedtime. She slept with a nightlight on and had never had a sleepover away from home.

She had to be terrified out of her mind.

"We'll find her," Brayden said softly.

She wanted to believe him. She had to.

Needing a distraction, she asked Brayden about his family. "How many brothers do you have?"

"There's four of us," Brayden said. "Harrison is the oldest and sheriff of Tumbleweed. Lucas is second in line. Then Dex, then me." He hesitated, his eyes darkening. "We had a little sister named Chrissy, but lost her when she was ten."

Mila frowned. "What happened? Or do you not want to talk about it?"

He shrugged, but averted his gaze and looked out

the window. A fall breeze stirred the trees, sending an array of colorful leaves to the ground. Yet dark clouds hovered, adding a dismal gray cast to the sky.

"I'm surprised you didn't see the news story about it. She disappeared one night when our parents were gone. For years, we had no idea what had happened. But a few months ago, we discovered the truth." He paused. "Unfortunately, she was dead and had been since the day she'd gone missing."

"I'm so sorry," Mila said. "That must have been difficult on you and your family."

"It was," Brayden admitted in a low voice. "My brothers and I all blamed ourselves because we were supposed to watch Chrissy that night. My mother went into a depression after she disappeared, but never gave up hope that we'd find her." His voice cracked. "Then my father just up and left."

"He abandoned your family?" Mila asked.

Brayden nodded. "We haven't heard from him in years."

How could a man desert his sons and wife, especially when they needed him?

"What about your family?" Brayden asked. "Any siblings?"

Mila's stomach twisted as she saw the ME and a crime worker carry Roberta out on a stretcher. Because Roberta was enclosed in a body bag, Mila couldn't see the physical damage done to her friend, but her experience filled in the blanks.

Thankfully, no neighbors were home to see what was going on, and the media hadn't shown up.

"Mila?"

She dragged her gaze from the van as the ME closed the back door.

"No. I was adopted but lost both of my adopted parents a while back."

"Charlotte mentioned a little about your past. I'm sorry about your birth mother," Brayden said.

She shook off his concern. "I was lucky to have the two parents I had. My mother traveled to foreign countries to help children in need. I wanted to follow in her footsteps, and I did." Another reason she'd had to take Izzy from Carina—she wanted to give Izzy the same chance that her adopted parents had given her.

Lucas appeared outside her house, then drove back to them.

She tensed as he got out and approached them. Brayden opened the door and stepped out. Mila wanted to know what was going on, so she joined them.

"Are you ready to talk to that sketch artist?" Lucas asked.

Mila's stomach knotted. She still didn't trust anyone. "I was thinking that perhaps I could work with Charlotte, that way we don't have to involve anyone else."

A muscle ticked in Lucas's jaw. "I suppose we could do that."

"About my clothes?" Mila asked.

"Tell me what you'll want and I'll go in," Brayden offered.

Mila squared her shoulders. "I'll get them. I'm a doctor, I've seen blood before."

"This is different," Lucas said.

"I'll be fine," Mila said sharply. "It won't take long."

"I'll go with her," Brayden said.

Lucas nodded. "I'll stand guard outside the house."

BRAYDEN ESCORTED MILA INSIDE. "There's probably fingerprint dust all over everything. Just ignore it, and we'll have a cleanup crew in here ASAP."

Mila gripped her hands together. "She was in the kitchen?"

Brayden nodded. "Your room and Izzy's are blood free."

Unease flittered through Mila's eyes. No matter what he'd said, she probably felt responsible for the nanny's death and would carry guilt with her for a long time.

He understood that himself. Even after they'd found Chrissy's body a few months ago, he couldn't shake the fact that if he hadn't encouraged her to sneak out with him and go to that swimming hole where Lucas and the other teens were celebrating the end of the school year, she'd still be alive.

He was eleven at the time and wanted to explore the caves at the edge of the mountain. He fell and hurt his ankle, and lost sight of Chrissy. Later he rode his bike home thinking she'd be there, but she hadn't shown up.

Instead…

He couldn't go back to the past.

Mila needed him to focus now. He hadn't been able to save his little sister. He had to save Mila's daughter.

He opened the door for her, and they walked inside. The scent of blood and death filled the air. He'd seen crime scenes before, but this one felt more personal because he knew a child had been kidnapped in the process.

Mila might be accustomed to blood and gore in the hospital and operating room, but a crime scene was different—violence at its worst. And this one involved her little girl.

She exhaled and walked quickly past the kitchen, then hurried to her bedroom. He followed but remained at the door to keep watch, offering her privacy to absorb the shock and gather her thoughts.

Her experience in crisis situations was evident as she lifted her chin and went straight to work. She pulled an overnight bag from the closet and threw in a couple of pairs of jeans, shirts and a sweater. She opened her dresser drawer, and he noticed pajamas and underwear, so he turned to face the wall.

He didn't need to see or even think about what kind of underwear the pretty doctor wore. But his imagination took him there anyway, and he pictured her curves encased in thin black lace.

His body hardened at the image in his mind. Dammit, he could not fantasize about her. Not when finding her child took priority.

He scrubbed his hand over his eyes to clear his mind. Footsteps sounded behind him, then her voice.

"I'm ready."

He turned toward her and took the overnight bag from her. "I need my phone."

"Your phone is still being held in evidence, but we'll get you another one and set it up with the same number."

She glanced inside Izzy's room. Her composure slipped slightly at the disarray.

"She always sleeps with her stuffed monkey. She named him Brownie," Mila said. "She cries without him."

His chest clenched. "I know this is difficult," Brayden said. "But you have to stay strong, Mila. She'll need you when we bring her home."

MILA DUCKED INSIDE Izzy's room to retrieve the monkey, but she couldn't find it. Maybe she had it with her. At least the stuffed animal would give her comfort.

The sight of her daughter's empty, unmade bed tore her heart in two. Thoughts of what DiSanti did to young girls threatened, but she staunchly pushed them away. Izzy was only three. He wouldn't touch her that way.

At least not now. When she was a teenager though…

No, they'd get Izzy back.

She hung on to that thought, grabbed the pink blanket Izzy slept with, then some extra clothes and one of her dolls and stuffed them in the overnight bag.

She crossed back to the door where Brayden was waiting. They walked through the house in silence and met Lucas at the door.

"Do you want me to follow you to the ranch?" Lucas asked.

Brayden shook his head. "I'll take her from here. Just get her a phone in case DiSanti's men try to reach her."

Mila hesitated. In spite of the fact that Lucas had arrested her, the Hawk family seemed caring and determined to do the right thing. Even Lucas wasn't bad—he'd saved those teenagers and married Charlotte. He'd even arrested her to stop DiSanti once and for all. How could she fault him for that?

"Get me the phone, then take me to a hotel, Brayden," Mila said. "I don't want to put your family in danger."

The Hawk men exchanged a look, then Lucas spoke.

"Let us worry about the family," Lucas said. "Harrison can arrange extra protection for the ranch."

"But what if DiSanti discovers I'm there?" Mila asked.

Brayden took her arm. "Trust me, no one will know."

There was that word again. *Trust.*

She climbed into Brayden's SUV and looked out the window as he drove. Once they left the outskirts of Austin, the city gave way to beautiful countryside. Farms and ranches and wide-open spaces.

All places Izzy would love.

Tears pricked her eyes, but she blinked them away and grappled for courage.

Once Izzy was safe, she'd see that DiSanti paid.

Exhaustion and stress wore her down, and she closed her eyes. The next time she opened them, Brayden was crossing under a sign for Hawk's Landing.

She blinked in awe at the acres and acres of beautiful land. Barns and stables dotted the hills, and horses galloped across open pastures. In the distance, she spotted a big rambling farmhouse with a huge wraparound porch, then a couple of rustic cabins nearby.

"This is where you grew up?" she asked.

Brayden smiled. "Yeah, except for losing my sister, it was pretty great."

She imagined it was. "Do you and your brothers all ride and work the ranch?"

"We all ride. As teenagers, my brothers and I worked the ranch. Dexter has a place in Austin for his PI business, but he also handles the equine operation and has added horses this last year since Charlotte's students came to live with my mom." He gestured toward a dirt road that led to acreage lush with more pastures. "My brother Harrison and his wife live up there." He pointed the opposite direction toward more land that stretched far and wide. "Lucas and Charlotte live over there. Harrison's wife, Honey, owns a renovation business. She remodeled the cabin they moved into as well as the one Lucas and Charlotte chose."

"And yours?"

He shrugged. "Maybe someday. For now, it's just me, so no need for fuss."

"The ranch is amazing," Mila said, and meant it.

The smile that lit Brayden's eyes was so sincere that it warmed her inside.

"Like Dex, I have a place in the city, too. But I keep a cabin on the ranch for when I'm home." He slowed as they neared the turnoff for the main farmhouse. "Do you want to meet my mother and the girls?"

She shook her head. "I don't want to involve them in any of this. I'd never forgive myself if one of them were hurt because of me."

"Mila," Brayden said in a husky voice. "My mother is housing four girls who were kidnapped by DiSanti. My family is as invested in seeing DiSanti brought down as anyone."

"I appreciate you saying that," Mila said. "But I spent the night in a jail cell last night. I need to clean up."

"Of course. I'm sorry. I'm not trying to pressure you." He veered down another dirt road, the SUV bouncing over ruts as he passed a pond and headed up a hill. To the right, she spotted a cowboy riding across the pasture, corralling some horses toward the barn. Instantly her nerves went on edge.

"Who is that?"

Brayden laid his hand over hers. "Relax, Mila. That's our foreman. He's the reason I went into law."

Mila narrowed her eyes. "What happened?"

"He was framed," Brayden said. "I was a cop at the time and realized the injustice, so I decided to study law to help him. I did, and now he works here."

Mila licked her suddenly dry lips. Brayden was definitely one of the good guys. A rancher at heart, a lawyer who represented the underdog.

She'd accept his help, then she'd get out of his life so she wouldn't cause him or his family any more trouble than she already had.

Then and only then would her secret about Izzy be safe.

JADE KRAMER WRAPPED the little girl Izzy in a soft blanket, then cradled her close and rocked her to sleep.

The poor little angel had cried so much her eyelids were swollen and red and she'd finally exhausted herself into sleep.

She wanted her mommy. Who could blame her?

She'd wanted her own mother when DiSanti had first brought her here, and she'd been fourteen years old.

That was over a year ago, and she still missed her family. She couldn't make herself believe that her father had sold her to DiSanti as he said.

Sure, she'd believed him at first.

But living on his compound and being bartered like cattle had taught her a lot.

DiSanti was a liar and a bastard, and he didn't care who he hurt as long as he made money.

The little girl stirred again, her tiny body trembling as she fought in her sleep.

She rocked her back and forth and stroked her hair away from her forehead, then kissed her cheek and began to sing her a lullaby. It was one her mama used to sing to help her fall asleep at night.

God, she missed her mama. Wished she could go back to being an innocent kid again. But those days were long gone.

Izzy whimpered and clawed at her arm, but Jade held her close and whispered sweet nothings in the child's ear.

She had to keep her quiet. DiSanti didn't like anyone to mess up his plans. She'd seen what he could do when he was angry.

It wouldn't matter that Izzy was just a tiny, innocent baby.

He'd give orders to get rid of her without blinking an eye.

Hot tears burned Jade's eyes. She'd long ago stopped crying for herself and for what the men had done to her. Her life no longer mattered.

But this little girl's did.

She'd do anything to keep her alive.

Chapter Eleven

Brayden considered putting Mila in one of the guest cabins, but he didn't want to leave her alone, so he took her to his place. She was so independent and frightened for her daughter that if she heard from DiSanti, she might attempt to face him by herself.

And that would be dangerous for her and Izzy. DiSanti was going to kill both of them anyway.

Unless they stopped him.

"This is nice," she said as he showed her through the kitchen/living room/dining area, then to the guest bedroom and bath. "Take your time. I'll run up to the house and see if Mother made dinner and grab us a plate."

She rolled her shoulders, obviously exhausted and worried. He waited until she ducked into the bathroom, then he locked up and drove to the farmhouse.

He spotted the teens outside with the foreman brushing down the horses, then found his mother cleaning up in the kitchen. The scent of homemade soup and corn bread lingered.

"Lucas called and explained that you have a guest." His mother's concerned gaze penetrated his. "Is there anything I can do to help?"

Brayden offered his mother a smile.

"If you have leftovers, we could use some. We haven't eaten all day."

A smile brightened his mother's face. They could always count on Ava Hawk for a good meal. "I'll pack up some soup and corn bread. And I have a fresh pumpkin pie."

His stomach growled. "Sounds wonderful."

She bustled around scooping soup into a container, then wrapped up two big chunks of corn bread, covered half a pie with foil and placed everything in an insulated bag for him to carry home.

He gave her a kiss on the cheek. "Thanks, Mom."

She hugged him tight. "Take care and be safe, son. And save that doctor's little girl."

"We're going to," he said, praying he didn't let Mila down.

His phone was buzzing with a text as he got back in his SUV. Lucas.

Charlotte and I are on our way. Bringing a phone for Mila.

He texted okay, then sped back toward his place. Hopefully, Mila's description of DiSanti's new face would enable them to track down the bastard and put him away.

Mila SHOWERED QUICKLY, grateful to finally clean the stench of DiSanti's blood from her skin. But she couldn't wash away the vile odor of what he was.

She quickly threw on a pair of sweats and towel dried

her hair. By the time she emerged, she heard the door opening and Brayden calling her name.

She met him in the kitchen, where he was ladling vegetable soup into two bowls.

"My mom sent this and some corn bread and pie. I hope you like soup."

"It smells heavenly," Mila said. She couldn't remember when she'd last eaten. A breakfast bar the morning before she went to the clinic, then she'd skipped lunch while she was working on DiSanti. They'd offered her food in that cell, but she'd been too sick to her stomach to keep anything down.

They carried the bowls and corn bread to the farm table, and he returned with silverware and napkins.

"Would you like a drink? I have beer and bourbon, and I might have a bottle of wine left from Charlotte and Lucas's wedding."

"Water is good," Mila said. She had to keep her wits about her.

He poured them both glasses of ice water and sat down across from her at the table.

She was so hungry that she practically inhaled the meal. He was quiet, too, as they ate.

Then he dished them slices of pumpkin pie that made her mouth water. "Your mother is a good cook."

"She loves it. We used to grow our own vegetables when I was young, before we lost Chrissy." He shrugged. "She's talking about having a garden next summer since she'll have the girls to help."

"Giving those girls a home is admirable."

"Yeah, my mom is something else. Strong…like you."

Their gazes locked, tension simmering between

them. She'd thought she was strong until she saw that gun at Izzy's head. Then she'd wanted to crumble.

"Charlotte and Lucas are on their way," Brayden said as he brewed a pot of coffee.

Fatigue knotted her shoulders, but she knew she had to face them.

If she could help find DiSanti, it would lead to Izzy.

A knock sounded on the door and Brayden rushed to get it. Lucas entered, then Charlotte.

Although Mila hadn't seen her friend in years, the connection they shared was still there. Charlotte raced over to her, and they hugged.

"God, Mila, I'm glad you're okay, but I know you're worried sick about your daughter."

Mila leaned into her friend and accepted her comfort, although the sincere worry in Charlotte's tone brought fresh tears to her eyes.

When they finally pulled apart, Charlotte cradled Mila's hands in hers. "I understand you're scared, but Lucas and the Hawk men are the best there is. They'll find your little girl."

Mila offered Charlotte a sympathetic smile. "I heard about what happened to you and your students. I'm so sorry for what you went through."

Charlotte squeezed her hands. "It was difficult, but I survived. The girls are happy now that they have a home at Hawk's Landing. Ava has given them love and emotional support." She glanced at Lucas with a smile. "I also met my husband from the ordeal. He's been amazing."

"I'm so glad you found happiness," Mila said sincerely. Charlotte had suffered ridicule as a child because of her port-wine birthmark. Mila's adopted mother had removed the birthmark, the first step in helping Charlotte recover her self-esteem.

"So," Charlotte said. "I understand that we need to sketch what that horrible DiSanti looks like now."

"Yes, we might as well get started."

Brayden offered coffee, but Charlotte declined, and so did Mila. She was already shaky. Caffeine would only make it worse.

Charlotte removed a large sketch pad and arranged her supplies on the coffee table between the two wing chairs facing the fireplace.

Lucas gave her a phone. "You have the same number as before, so if DiSanti calls, he won't realize the difference. We placed a trace on the phone. Keep him on the line as long as possible so we can get a location."

She nodded that she understood, then joined Charlotte.

Charlotte gestured toward a photo of DiSanti. "I thought the picture would be a good starting point. Then you can tell me how you altered features and I can draw them in for a composite."

WHILE MILA AND Charlotte collaborated on the sketch of DiSanti, Brayden and Lucas convened at the kitchen table.

Lucas spread out a map, then removed three photographs of different men from a folder and laid them in a row.

"Right now we have made connections from DiSanti to each of these men, although we don't have enough evidence to make arrests."

He tapped the first picture, a dark-haired, dark-skinned man in a slick suit with a mole beside his upper lip. "This is Juan Andres. We believe he's the major connection in Colombia and is also part of the drug cartel. So far though, no one has or will speak out against him. The two people who tried are dead. Tortured and butchered and left hanging in their village to make a statement to anyone else who contemplated turning to the authorities. Another problem is corrupt law officials who turn a blind eye for money."

Disgusting.

Lucas continued, all business. "Next is a man named Lem Corley. He owns a ranch between here and Austin. Corley's operation has grown by leaps and bounds the past five years."

"Have you questioned him?"

"Not yet, I'm working on obtaining enough information for warrants. Corley also owns a second property near Juarez. We suspect he's taking payoffs for smuggling the girls through an underground tunnel across the border from the US to Mexico. From there, it's easier to send them wherever they want."

Brayden silently cursed.

"The third is a shocker because it's close to home."

Brayden's pulse jumped. "Isn't that Jameson Beck, the candidate for mayor?"

"Exactly. We've suspected he was corrupt as a councilman, but he has money and charm and has fooled people into voting for him. If he wins this bid as mayor, there's no telling how much damage he'll do."

Brayden's mind raced. Even when they found Izzy,

Lucas still had his work cut out to make DiSanti's empire fall apart.

Charlotte and Mila stood and walked outside on the back deck.

Lucas poured himself more coffee and Brayden followed.

As usual, Lucas's eyes assessed him. His brother had an intimidating air, which worked well with felons and the evil dregs that he hunted down.

But he hated it when Lucas aimed those suspicious eyes toward him.

"Do you think Mila has told you everything?" Lucas asked.

Did he?

Brayden grabbed his coffee mug from the counter and blew into the steaming brew. "Yes."

Was Lucas going to remind him of the time when he fell for a client's innocent act?

"She's never married?" Lucas asked.

Irritation knifed through him. "It's not uncommon for women to have children without marriage, Lucas."

His brother sighed. "I know that. But what about the little girl's father? Did she tell you who he is?"

Brayden shook his head no. "He's dead."

A tense silence stretched between them. "And you believe her?"

"I have no reason not to. Now let's look at the facts. A dead man has nothing to do with Izzy now."

"What if she's lying?" Lucas said.

Brayden didn't want to believe that Mila would lie to him. But he'd been fooled before by another woman.

"Hell, Brayden," Lucas said. "Use your charms—do

whatever it takes to find out his name. For all we know, he could be working with DiSanti."

MILA FROZE AT the sound of Lucas's question. Brayden told Lucas exactly what she'd said.

But Lucas wanted more.

He would probably keep digging away until he discovered the truth.

She couldn't let that happen.

"Mila, are you all right?" Charlotte asked.

She jerked her attention back to Charlotte and nodded. "Just thinking about Izzy. Wondering if she's hungry or if she slept last night. If she thinks I've forgotten her or knows that I'm looking."

Charlotte stroked Mila's shoulder. "Izzy knows you love her. She'll hang on to that." Charlotte glanced at the Hawk men, a tenderness in her eyes that Mila envied.

The Hawks had a close-knit, loving family here. They'd endured hard times and pulled through them together. And this ranch—it was spectacular. It offered a child a great place to grow up and a safe haven from the dangers of the world.

Not that her childhood had been bad. Her parents had helped save the world. But they'd moved and traveled so much that she'd never called a place home.

She wanted that for Izzy.

Even if she had to forgo her trips abroad, she'd give Izzy that sense of stability and home.

Charlotte took the sketch to Lucas. Both men studied it as if memorizing every detail.

"Basically, I removed his scar, then gave him cheek implants, lip fillers, a nose job and eyelid lifts," Mila

said. "It'll take time for the swelling to go down and
the redness to fade, but he'll be handsome and charming, and no one will know there's a monster lurking
beneath that slick face."

The fact that she'd helped him achieve that made
bile rise to her throat.

"Thank you for the description," Lucas said.

Mila folded her arms. "Are you going to keep your
promise about airing it?"

Lucas gave a clipped nod, then flipped on the TV.
"I gave an interview before I came here. It should be
airing any minute."

They grew quiet as a young brunette anchorwoman
spoke into the mike. "Last night the FBI and local police arrested Austin plastic surgeon Dr. Mila Manchester for allegedly helping a wanted felon Arman DiSanti
escape. Authorities have been searching for DiSanti for
months in relation to a sex trafficking ring called the
Shetland operation." She gestured toward a screen. "I
spoke with Special Agent Lucas Hawk earlier today regarding the arrest. Here's what he had to say."

The camera focused on Lucas. "While it is true, we
arrested Dr. Manchester for allegedly conspiring to help
DiSanti escape authorities, Dr. Manchester has refused
to cooperate with us or reveal anything about DiSanti
and his operation. Nor did she divulge the man's whereabouts, his plans or his new face."

Mila clenched her hands by her side. Lucas had kept
his promise, at least regarding the media.

She just hoped DiSanti bought the story. And that
his men took the bait and gave her a call.

Chapter Twelve

Mila had to keep her secrets safe. If Brayden and Lucas knew the truth about Izzy being DiSanti's daughter, Lucas might lock her up. They might even accuse her of kidnapping, and then she might go to prison.

Lucas approached her, his look suspicious. "Dr. Manchester—"

"Please call me Mila."

Charlotte's presence comforted her in the face of Lucas's distrust.

"All right, Mila," Lucas said. "Tell me why DiSanti came to you for help."

She chewed the inside of her cheek. "Because I'm a plastic surgeon," she said, stating the obvious.

Irritation lined Lucas's face. "But why *you*? There are other plastic surgeons who could have performed the surgery."

She shrugged. "I don't know. Maybe he, or one of his people, read about me in an article featuring my work with needy children."

Lucas arched a brow. "Had you met DiSanti before? Or done work on him prior to this?"

"No, we'd never met." That part was true.

"DiSanti is from Colombia," Lucas pointed out. "You've traveled there to perform surgeries?"

Mila couldn't lie when he could easily check her schedule. "Twice. My mother also worked at a free clinic in Colombia at one time."

Maybe that would distract him from thinking about her, and Izzy's father.

Lucas narrowed his eyes. "Did you go with her?"

She nodded. "She was the reason I chose plastic surgery and work with Doctors Without Borders."

Charlotte rubbed Mila's arm. "She was a hero to me, that's for sure."

Lucas hesitated, his gaze softening as he looked at his wife.

Then he turned back to Mila. "Was it possible that DiSanti knew your mother?"

"She never mentioned his name to me. And if she'd known what kind of man he was, she certainly wouldn't have helped him. Her work focused on children and teenagers." Although it was possible that DiSanti had heard of her mother, and that he linked her to Mila.

"Let me ask you something else," Lucas said. "When you and your mother were in Colombia, did you hear about DiSanti and what he was doing? Was there talk or rumors about sex trafficking?"

Mila strained to remember. "I suppose, but I was only twelve at the time and didn't fully comprehend the details. I do recall that guards watched the clinic, and I was warned to stay close." A shudder coursed up her spine. "A couple of times, rape victims were brought in. Those frightened me because the girls were so young and traumatized."

Lucas studied her for a long moment, then seemed to accept what she said. At least for the moment. "Let me see the sketch again," Lucas said.

Charlotte handed the drawing to him, and Lucas scrutinized the features. "Did DiSanti or his men say anything while they were in your clinic?"

"Other than threatening my daughter?" Mila asked with a hint of sarcasm to her voice.

"I know that was harrowing," Lucas said. "But think about it? Maybe you overheard them discuss where they were going to take DiSanti to recover."

"If I knew where he was, I'd tell you." Mila rubbed her temple in thought. "All I remember is being so terrified that they'd hurt Izzy that I just did what they said. I cautioned them that I usually performed extensive plastic surgery in steps, but they insisted everything had to be completed that day."

Lucas removed a manila envelope from inside his jacket, and then took out a picture. "We took this from your house. Is this one of the latest pictures of your daughter?"

Mila traced a shaky finger over Izzy's innocent face. Her heart squeezed at the picture of Izzy sitting atop that pony. She'd been so excited about her first horse-back riding lesson. "That was in the summer. I took Izzy camping, and we made s'mores over the campfire, and slept under the stars." She bit her lip. "She was so happy that day."

"I'd like to issue an Amber Alert for her," Lucas said. "That is, if you agree."

Mila looked at Charlotte for advice. Yet the threat to her daughter rang in her ears. If they released a photograph, DiSanti and his men would know that she'd talked.

She shook her head. "Not yet."

Lucas sighed. "But if we don't hear from DiSanti's men by tomorrow, we should release it to the public. I probably don't have to tell you that with every hour and every day that a child is missing, the chances of recovering them grow slimmer."

Mila swallowed hard.

Charlotte tugged at Lucas's arm. "Why don't we let Mila get some sleep? Maybe she'll remember more once she's rested."

"If anything comes to mind, call me." He squeezed her arm. "Hang in there, Mila. We'll find your daughter."

His tender encouragement made emotions well in her throat.

Lucas and Charlotte left, and Mila went to look out the window. It was dark again. Nighttime.

No word about her daughter or where she was. Or even if she was safe.

She gripped the phone Lucas had left for her, walked outside onto the porch, sank into one of the porch rockers and willed it to ring.

BRAYDEN CLEANED UP the kitchen, tension lingering. Mila pushed the porch swing back and forth, her hand clutching that cell phone.

She'd spent last night in jail without Izzy. Tonight, she'd spend it alone again.

Something about his brother's conversation with

Mila troubled him. He sensed she was holding something back.

But what? Everything she'd told them about her mother was inspiring. And easy to check.

DiSanti was a good fifteen years older than Mila. He could have easily met her mother when she traveled to Colombia. He could also have seen Mila and read about her in the news. It made sense.

Lucas wanted him to find out about Izzy's father.

Frustrated, he settled in front of his laptop and sent Dexter an email giving him the names of the three men the FBI suspected to be involved with DiSanti's operation.

He asked Dex to send him everything he had on all three men.

He'd crossed paths with Jameson Beck before on the job. He'd heard rumors that the man was corrupt. That he had huge financial support from an unknown source.

Beck was slick, charming and made promises left and right to the public to win their votes.

Brayden didn't know the rancher Corley personally, but he and Dex could check him out together.

Beck was all his though.

Brayden accessed his personal number from his contact list, so he called it. The phone rang four times then went to voice mail. He left a message saying it was urgent, and that he needed to speak to him right away.

He hung up, hoping Beck would return his call tonight.

The next two hours crawled by. He researched everything he could find on persons of interest in the sex trafficking trade. Two arrests caught his attention, and he texted Harrison and asked him to go to the prison and question the inmates. They might be able to offer a lead as to where DiSanti and his men were hiding out.

Or if DiSanti had another connection in the States.

Antsy that he couldn't take action tonight, he walked outside to join Mila. He was frustrated—she must be going out of her mind.

She gave him a brief glance, then returned to staring out at the ranch. Normally he'd be bragging about their operation and how far they'd come this past year in updating the ranching side of the business.

But tonight, all he could think about was Mila and the sadness and fear in her eyes.

SOMETIME IN THE wee hours of the morning, Mila finally fell into an exhausted sleep.

She dreamed about the surgery.

She was on her feet for hours. Long stressful hours when she could barely focus for worrying about what Izzy was going through.

Her head throbbed and her feet ached. Sweat poured down the side of her face. She was so thirsty she had to pause for a quick sip of water.

"What are you doing?" one of the men barked.

"I need water," she said, then grabbed a bottle from the side table.

He kept his gun aimed at her. "Get back to it, Doc. If you try to pull anything or if the cops show up, you'll never see your kid again."

Rage heated her blood. She wanted to throw something at him, take that gun and turn it on him.

But she was a doctor, not a killer.

Although if they hurt Izzy, she might forget her oath.

She guzzled half the water bottle, then wiped her forehead with a cloth and returned to work. With every maneuver of the scalpel to alter his looks so he could walk away free, she imagined digging the blade into his cold, cold heart.

Voices echoed from the side. Concern flickered in one of the men's eyes as he answered a phone call. He motioned to the other man, and they surrounded her.

"Hurry up, we need to move."

"I need more time," Mila said. "What you're putting him through is dangerous."

"His choice," the brute said with a wave of his gun.

"I can't in good conscience finish if his blood pressure drops again."

"Just do your job. We have a place set up for his recovery."

"I can't work 24/7," Mila protested. "My hands aren't steady when I haven't slept."

"You'll have help and supplies where we're going," the man snapped.

"He's not up for travel," Mila argued.

The men conversed in Spanish for several seconds. Short, clipped angry words. She'd picked up a few phrases but wasn't fluent.

But she thought they said something about a medical facility close by.

Another clinic? A hospital?

The man with the radio jammed the gun at her chest. "Finish and do it now. We have to go."

Mila jerked awake, her heart racing. For a moment, she was so disoriented she thought she was back in the clinic operating room. But the curtain in the room was flapping, the soft whir of the furnace rumbling.

She glanced around, clutched the bedding in her clammy hands and blinked to focus. No, not in the clinic or her house.

At Hawk's Landing. Brayden's cabin.

She pushed the covers aside, then padded to the door. A dim light burned from the desk in the corner of the den. Brayden was slumped over the desk snoring lightly.

She tiptoed into the room, which was bathed in early morning sunlight shimmering through the French doors leading to the porch. Dawn was just breaking the sky.

Wrapping her arms around herself, she padded over to him and laid her hand on his shoulder.

"Brayden?" she whispered.

He startled, then jerked his head and looked up at her. "Yeah?"

"I remembered something. They said they had a place with medical supplies set up for DiSanti to recover. I think it was close to the clinic."

Chapter Thirteen

Brayden sat upright and rubbed his hand over his eyes. "Did they say where it was?"

Mila ran a hand through her tangled hair. Flannel pajamas be damned. Sleepy eyed with those unruly strands draping her shoulders, she looked young and sexy.

Not a good thought, man.

"Not specifically," Mila said, her voice riddled with frustration. "They were speaking in Spanish. I'm not fluent, but I understand a few phrases and words from our trips abroad."

Needing a distraction from his earlier thoughts, he stood, walked over to the kitchen and started a pot of coffee.

"Did they mention a direction they were going? A landmark?"

Mila pinched the bridge of her nose. "It sounded like they said something about a corral."

Brayden frowned. They were in Texas, a land rich with ranches, farmland and corrals.

He poured her a cup of coffee and himself a mug, then offered cream and sugar.

"Black," she said, and thanked him.

He carried his coffee to his desk, then checked his phone for messages. Beck still hadn't returned his call. He checked his email next and had one from Dexter listing a property that Jameson Beck owned that he thought they should search.

He sent his brother a text asking him to look for locations that might involve a medical setting, old doctor's office, abandoned hospital or lab, using the word *corral*.

Dex sent him a quick response that he was on it.

"Hopefully, Dex will get back to us about the corral. I'm going to talk to Jameson Beck."

Mila sipped her coffee. "What does he have to do with this?"

"He may be involved with DiSanti's operation," Brayden said.

Mila looked perplexed. "Jameson Beck is supposed to be helping citizens, not exploiting them."

"If we prove he's involved," Brayden said, "everyone will know exactly what he's done. Not only will his political career be over, but he'll serve time."

"I'm going with you," Mila said.

Brayden hesitated. "I'm not sure that's a good idea. I haven't told Lucas—"

"I don't care," Mila said. "DiSanti's people still haven't contacted me. If Beck is involved and knows what's happening with my daughter, then he should have to face me."

She had a point. It might be easier for Beck to blow him off, but not so easy when Mila made the situation personal.

"All right," Brayden said. "But let me do the talking."

Mila agreed, although determination flared in her eyes. "I'll get dressed."

He rushed to shower himself. Jameson Beck could be an imposing man. He wanted to present himself as an equal.

But if he had anything to do with Mila's daughter being taken, those kid gloves would come off.

MILA STUDIED JAMESON BECK with a skeptical eye. She'd always considered him a slick, cunning politician. He was impeccably dressed, hair groomed, teeth postcard white. He said the correct things and smoothed ruffled feathers with locals over unemployment, issues facing the ranchers and taxes.

He pretended to be an advocate for the lower income although he sported an expensive foreign car and the cost of his Italian loafers would go a long way toward feeding the impoverished.

Nerves pricked Mila's spine. Beck shook both their hands, invited them into his office and offered coffee. But her stomach was twisted so tightly she could barely swallow water.

She certainly didn't intend to swallow his lies if he dodged their questions.

And what if he was conspiring with DiSanti and tipped him off that she was cooperating with the police?

"I received your message late last night," Beck commented. "You said it was urgent."

"It is. I'm assuming you saw the news story about Dr. Manchester's arrest," Brayden said. "I'm representing her."

Beck's gray eyes showed no reaction. "I'm afraid I

didn't see the story," Beck said. "I was out of pocket all day yesterday and didn't get in until late last night."

Mila didn't believe him. In his position, he had people who kept him informed of what was happening in his city. With the upcoming election, he could pounce on anything juicy or topical and bend it to impress his constituents.

"Dr. Manchester was forced at gunpoint to perform surgery on DiSanti, a man suspected of spearheading the Shetland operation. You are familiar with that, aren't you?"

Brayden's biting tone seemed to raise Beck's hackles, but he quickly masked a reaction.

Beck rolled an expensive pen between his fingers. "Of course. I believe your brother made some arrests a few months ago and recovered four missing girls who'd been abducted by that group."

"That's correct." Brayden used a calm voice. "We need your help. If you know anything about DiSanti and his whereabouts, it's important that you tell us."

Beck leaned back in his desk chair, a picture of calm. "I wish I could help you, but I'm afraid I can't."

"Can't or won't?" Brayden asked, his voice challenging.

Beck clicked the pen. "I represent the people, Mr. Hawk. I would never associate with someone involved in illegal activities."

Brayden stood and leaned his hands on Beck's desk. "We both know that's a lie. Now, listen to me. I'm not after you. All I want is information about DiSanti and where he's hiding."

Anger slashed Beck's eyes. "I told you that I'm not involved with him."

"Maybe not," Brayden barked. "But if you're connected with someone who is, then tell me what you do know."

Beck buttoned his suit jacket. "I've asked and answered your question. Now it's time for you to leave."

Mila couldn't stand it any longer. She lurched up from her chair. "Mr. Beck, this man not only abducts and sells young women as sex slaves, but his people kidnapped my three-year-old little girl." Her voice broke. She snatched a picture from her wallet, a candid of Izzy at Christmas holding her baby doll. "Her name is Izzy," Mila said. "She's three, and she's afraid of the dark, and she likes macaroni and cheese and rainbows and ice cream."

A vein throbbed in his neck.

Mila gave him an imploring look. "If you know where he's holding her, please tell me."

His gaze met hers. His was full of steel, although a twinge of something akin to worry flickered in his eyes. Worry for himself or for her daughter?

He exhaled. "I'm sorry, Dr. Manchester. I hope you find her."

The calmness in his tone infuriated her even more. He was lying. She sensed it and refused to let him off the hook.

She snatched him by the collar and jerked his face toward hers. She expected Brayden to yank her away, but he didn't.

"If he hurts her, and I find out you knew where she was and didn't help me," she said through gritted teeth, "worrying about winning the election won't be an issue."

His gaze shot to Brayden. "You need to calm your client, Mr. Hawk."

Mila shook him. "This is calm, Mr. Beck." Venom laced her tone. "I promise you that if I don't get my daughter back safe and sound, jail will be the least of your problems."

"You heard her threaten me," Beck said to Brayden.

Brayden shrugged. "I didn't hear anything of the sort."

Mila straightened and reluctantly released Beck.

Beck cleared his throat, his nostrils flaring. "The next time you want to talk to me, go through my attorney."

Brayden shot him a cynical smile. "Fine. I'm sure the residents of Austin will be interested in knowing that instead of helping us find a known sex trafficker and a missing child, that you lawyered up to protect your own ass."

Brayden didn't wait for a response. He took Mila's arm and they left the room.

Her heart hammered in her chest. Brayden Hawk was a formidable man and lawyer.

He was also one of the good guys, not like Beck, who was all show with a selfish, greedy side lurking beneath.

BRAYDEN'S PHONE BUZZED as he and Mila climbed back into his SUV. Dex.

He quickly connected. "I'm just leaving Beck's office. That bastard knows something, but he sure as hell isn't talking."

"I'll keep digging," Dex said. "I did find something though—at least I think I did. You said Mila mentioned something about a corral?"

"Like I said, they were speaking in Spanish, so she wasn't sure of the translation."

"I found an abandoned hospital in a small hole-in-the-wall town called O'Kade Corral," Dex said.

Brayden's pulse jumped. "Where is it?"

"Sending the address to your phone now," Dex said. "The town was built around some old mines, which was the reason for the hospital. But the mines yielded nothing, so the workers moved on and the town crumbled."

But it would provide a hiding spot for DiSanti during his recuperation.

Dex agreed to meet him there, and Brayden hung up, then glanced at the address Dex had sent. Mila was checking her own phone, willing it to ring again, he guessed.

Disappointment lined her face as she laid it back in her lap. "What's going on?"

Brayden explained about Dex's call. "The town isn't far from here."

Mila fastened her seat belt. "Let's go."

Brayden fastened his own seat belt, started the engine and veered into traffic. He wove through the downtown streets of Austin, then onto the highway leading out of the city.

Mila twisted her phone between her hands, constantly checking it as he raced down the highway. He considered calling Lucas, but he didn't want to waste Lucas's time if this was a wild-goose chase.

The city landscape gave way to farmland and ranches,

then he veered onto a narrow road that wove through miles and miles of nothing. The road was bumpy and filled with potholes, another sign that the area was deserted.

He maneuvered a turn, then spotted several small buildings in the distance. The town looked like a ghost town—a small building that had once been a mercantile, a bank, a diner and honky-tonk. All deserted, the buildings weathered, paint fading.

He scanned the streets and surrounding land for cars or signs indicating someone was here. A few pieces of rusted mining equipment had been left near the overgrown trails leading to the mines.

"It looks vacant," Mila said, disappointment tingeing her voice.

In the distance sat a larger building that could be the old hospital. A white van and an ambulance were parked near the building, half hidden by weeds and patchy shrubs.

Mila clutched his arm. "They were driving a van the night they brought DiSanti to the clinic."

Brayden pulled over between a clump of trees to wait on Dexter. The last thing he wanted was to alert DiSanti's men they were here before backup arrived.

If he got himself and Mila killed, he couldn't save Izzy.

He texted Dex to tell him to approach with caution and pull off where he'd parked. The air in the car felt charged with tension as they waited, Mila's anxiety palpable.

Five minutes passed, then Dex coasted up in his black pickup. He slowed and veered into the space beside Brayden and parked. Brayden removed his hand-gun from the locked dash and checked the magazine.

Both he and his brother eased their doors open and slid out, carefully closing them so they didn't make noise. Mila joined them, but Dexter and he exchanged understanding looks.

"Stay here while we take a look around," Brayden said.

"But if Izzy's there, she'll be scared and need me," Mila whispered.

Brayden gently touched her arm. "It's too danger-ous, Mila. Once we scout out the hospital, we'll let you know if it appears anyone is there. If DiSanti's here, we'll call Lucas for backup."

"But if Izzy's in there—"

"Rushing inside without a plan could work against us," Brayden said. "We have to play it smart. The most important thing is to get Izzy out safely."

Mila sighed and gripped the edge of the SUV. "Please find her, Brayden."

His heart stuttered. Dex's face twisted with emo-tions, as well.

"We'll do our best," Brayden said. "But I need you to stay in the SUV, lock the doors and keep down. If DiSanti has men watching or riding the property, we don't want them to see you."

Mila agreed, and he waited until she was locked in-side the vehicle, then he and Dexter headed through the woods toward the building.

Dex pulled binoculars from his pocket and focused on the van and ambulance first, then across the property.

He shook his head, indicating he didn't see movement.

Brayden gripped his gun at the ready, and they crossed behind some trees, taking cover as they moved toward the building.

Dex motioned that he'd check the side windows, while Brayden veered around the right to the back window near the parked ambulance.

Just as he grew close, something caught his eye.

A small stuffed monkey. It looked well-worn and loved, its ears frayed.

His throat closed. If it belonged to Izzy, she might be here.

Chapter Fourteen

Brayden stooped down, picked up the stuffed monkey, his heart clenching at the tattered ears. Izzy, or some child, had loved this little toy. It had probably given comfort.

He stuffed it inside his pocket and inched forward until he reached the back door, a metal one with a window covered to offer privacy to patients it had once served—or to hide whoever was inside.

Dex gave a low whistle from the side of the building and gestured that he couldn't see inside.

In fact, all the windows were covered.

Suspicious.

Brayden crept forward and gently turned the doorknob. Locked.

Dex appeared a second later. Brayden ignored the fact that his brother carried a lock-picking tool and that they had no warrant. If he had to, he'd say they thought they heard a child crying inside.

Dex picked the lock and turned the knob, pushing it open an inch at a time. Brayden peered through the opening. The interior was dark. Quiet.

His heart hammered.

Dex motioned for them to go inside, and Brayden slipped into the doorway. Dex kept his gun at the ready and went right, and they both paused to listen. A rattling sound. Wind whistling through the cracks in the windows.

No voices. No lights.

Still, they moved with caution in case DiSanti's men had been here and left a lookout guy to ambush them. He followed his brother down the hall, each checking rooms on the side of the hall. Exam rooms, a surgical wing, a pharmacy with glass cabinets that had once held drugs, a recovery room, then several patient rooms, two of which still housed hospital beds.

All empty.

Dex motioned to another room at the end, and he inched along behind Dex, both treading quietly until they reached the room. Brayden peered through the window of the door. Empty.

But it looked as if someone had been there recently.

He pushed open the door and stepped inside, waving Dexter to join him. The lights were off, so he pulled his flashlight from his pocket and shone it around the room.

Alcohol, blood stoppers and medical supplies filled a metal side table. Bloody clothes were stuffed into a bin next to a hospital bed that appeared to have recently been slept in. A sheet and blanket stained with blood were rumpled on top of the mattress, and a used syringe lay on another steel table.

"They're gone," Dexter said. "Do you think they knew we were coming?"

"I don't know how they could," Brayden said. "You only discovered this place today."

"Maybe one of them figured out that Mila overheard their conversation."

"I guess that's possible." Brayden's hand rubbed the stuffed monkey in his pocket, and he showed it to his brother. "Let's search the cabinets and closets in case Izzy was here."

Dex traded a worried look with him. If she was, and they thought Mila had ratted them out, they might have ditched her.

He prayed that wasn't the case, but DiSanti was the most ruthless man he'd ever encountered.

WHAT WAS TAKING so long?

Mila remained hidden, but the minutes dragged by, intensifying her anxiety. Had the Hawk men found something inside?

She turned and scanned the property for vehicles, but the place appeared deserted. Fresh tire marks marred the dirt leading up to the hospital, another set leading past the hospital to the opposite side.

Someone had been here recently, and they were gone. But where? What lay to the south?

She reached for the doorknob to go and look in that van herself, then remembered Brayden's warning.

Still jittery, she checked her phone. No text or phone call.

She logged in to her work email and checked messages at the clinic. Not that DiSanti would send her a message there. It would be too easy for the police to check.

Why hadn't they called? Lucas had announced that she wasn't cooperating.

Maybe she should ask Brayden and Lucas to set up a TV interview where she could make a public plea for her daughter's return. By now, DiSanti and his men could be hundreds of miles away.

If they had Izzy with them, she might never see her little girl again.

Panic robbed her breath. She reached for the door handle once more, but saw movement ahead.

Brayden and his brother Dexter exiting the building.

Disappointment swelled inside her. Izzy wasn't with them. They were no closer to getting her back than they had been before.

Lucas's statement taunted her. She'd read the statistics, too. Every minute, every hour, every day that they didn't find Mila's daughter diminished her chances of finding her alive.

Brayden halted by the van, opened the door and climbed inside while his brother searched the back of the ambulance. She held her breath as she waited, her patience waning when they finished and walked toward her.

She slipped from the SUV. "Did you find anything inside?"

Brayden's dark expression made her stomach knot. "They were here," he said. "There were bloody cloths and medical supplies spread out, but they're gone."

Mila gestured toward the tire tracks. "It looks like a vehicle left that way," she said.

Dex shone his light on the tracks to examine them.

Mila rocked back on the balls of her feet. "Brayden, was there any sign of Izzy?"

Brayden removed something from his jacket pocket and handed it toward her. "Is this hers?"

Mila nodded, then took the tiny monkey and pressed it to her chest.

BRAYDEN'S PHONE BUZZED. LUCAS.

"Was there any clue where?" Mila asked.

"I'm afraid not," Brayden said. "But DiSanti's men could have taken her to another location, maybe where they're holding other victims."

They'd kept Charlotte's students at an abandoned ranch off the grid. If Izzy was with other girls, she wouldn't be quite so terrified. Except they usually kept those girls drugged and incoherent.

There hadn't been reports of any abductions near Tumbleweed or Austin in the past few weeks, but DiSanti's people might be moving victims from other states through. Or they could be playing it more low-key, taking one victim at a time, choosing from runaways or girls without families who no one would report missing.

His phone buzzed again. "It's Lucas. I need to get this."

Mila leaned against the car while he walked a few feet away for privacy.

"Where are you?" Lucas asked.

Brayden braced himself for one of Lucas's big-brother lectures. But if they wanted to find DiSanti and Izzy, they had to work together, so he explained.

"Dammit, Brayden, why didn't you call me?" Lucas asked.

Because he didn't want to get his brother in trouble in case Dex and he straddled the law. "There wasn't time," Brayden said. "Besides, I didn't know if it would lead to anything. I want you working your end."

"I am," Lucas said. "But I can't do that if I have to worry about you going off on your own."

"I'm not alone," Brayden said.

Lucas exploded with a string of expletives. "Dex is with you?"

"Yes, but we haven't broken any laws, Lucas. Dex and I just checked out an abandoned hospital. DiSanti was here, but he's gone."

Lucas hissed between his teeth. "Any sign where they went from there?"

"No, but I found a stuffed toy indicating Mila's daughter was here."

"Dammit." Lucas paused, breath wheezing out. "I heard that you paid Jameson Beck a visit."

Brayden clenched his jaw. "Yeah, but he's not talking."

"I didn't expect him to. But our analyst traced one of his phone calls to an old inn in a small town about thirty miles south of Austin."

The tire tracks leading away from the hospital were headed south.

"Send me the address."

"Brayden, let me do this."

"Let's meet, Lucas. If Izzy's there, she'll need Mila." He lowered his voice so she couldn't hear. "And if Izzy's hurt or if there are other hostages, they might need medical attention."

A strained heartbeat passed. "I don't like it, but you're right."

He ended the call then went to tell Dexter and Mila the plan.

MILA TWISTED THE monkey in her hands as Brayden drove toward Cactus Grove, a small town south of Austin that drew tourists for its desertlike garden, variety of cacti and sagebrush. A local museum showcased the history of the wagon trains that used to travel through the town to Austin, and the town still boasted a working train station.

"Is Dexter coming?" Mila asked.

Brayden shook his head. "He's going to check with one of his CIs. Maybe he'll have information that can help."

"Does Lucas think DiSanti's in this town?" Mila asked.

Brayden shrugged. "It's possible. He traced a call from Beck to Cactus Grove. If DiSanti's operation is using the town as a holding place for trafficking and we can connect it to Beck, then we can use it as leverage to force Beck to talk."

Mila fidgeted with her phone. "Why haven't they called me, Brayden?"

Brayden clenched his jaw. "Maybe they're just regrouping."

Or maybe they'd left the country and taken Izzy with them.

The countryside flew past as Brayden sped down the road to Cactus Grove. The wind stirred the pines and sagebrush, flinging dust across the road in a brown fog.

As they approached the small town, traffic built

slightly, although compared to Austin they were in the wilderness. They passed the train station and museum, then a newer inn in town that was decked out for Thanksgiving. At the end of the square, an old-fashioned diner and a Western saloon invited customers to enjoy a taste of days gone by. Brayden parked in front of the town stage.

"What are you doing?" Mila asked.

"Waiting on Lucas."

Mila studied the wooden platform in front of them. "What is this place?"

"Every year the town performs a reenactment of a historical gunfight that occurred in the town a hundred years ago."

She tapped her foot, impatient as they waited on Lucas to arrive. A black sedan crawled by and slowed as if looking at them, then a dark gray Cadillac.

Lucas pulled up and motioned for them to join him in his sedan. When they climbed in, Lucas gave them both stern looks.

"I'm in charge here, so you two need to do as I say."

"Yes, sir," Brayden said with a tinge of irritation.

"I mean it, Brayden. I know you have experience, but I don't want either of you getting hurt."

"I don't give a damn about getting hurt," Mila said. "All I want is my daughter back."

"That's exactly what worries me," Lucas said with a frown.

Brayden raked a hand through his hair. "He's right, Mila. When we get there, you have to stay inside the car and remain hidden. If we find something, we'll come and get you. I promise."

Mila bit down on her lower lip and nodded. She'd been held at gunpoint by DiSanti's men. She knew what it was like to be powerless. The last thing she wanted was to get her daughter hurt or to die and leave Izzy without a mother.

Lucas started the engine, then turned onto a narrow road leading toward more farmland.

"There's an inn out here?" Mila asked.

Brayden nodded. "It was the original one and catered not only to tourists, but miners who still thought they might find gold in the mines. They abandoned the inn a couple of years ago when they built the new one by the train station. Made it easier for people to walk the town."

They passed several abandoned small cabins and a building that had probably once been used to store mining supplies, then she spotted the inn, an antebellum house with a big porch that looked homey and quaint.

Those abandoned buildings could be used to hold trafficking victims.

A black van was parked in back of the inn, an old pickup near the warehouse.

"We'll check the inn first, then those buildings," Lucas said.

Brayden gave Mila a pointed look. "I meant what I said. Stay put."

"I will," she said, her hand stroking the monkey's ears.

"If you see something, text me," Brayden said. He shocked her by slipping a small .22 into her hand.

She looked at the gun, not sure if she could use it. But an image of Izzy being held by that monster taunted her, and she knew she could shoot if it meant saving her daughter's life.

Lucas took the lead as the men climbed from the car and inched toward the inn.

She held her breath, praying for their safety and that they found Izzy before it was too late.

Time seemed to stand still. The tension thrumming through her made her feel sick inside.

Suddenly her phone buzzed. She startled, then glanced down at it. Brayden?

No.

A text. She opened it and gasped. A picture of her little girl huddled in a dark corner, teary eyed and terrified.

Then a message.

If you want to see your daughter again, ditch the cops. Will contact again with instructions.

Chapter Fifteen

Brayden approached the inn, his senses alert. Lucas motioned to let him take the lead, and Brayden did. Entering an unknown situation that could be an ambush was never his favorite part of police work.

He'd gotten spoiled by dealing with trouble and crime in the courtroom instead of on the front line. Although the law could be frustrating at times, too.

Seeing a guilty criminal released without being punished was infuriating and happened too often, while watching an innocent person go to prison was intolerable.

Lucas paused to listen at the door, his brows furrowed. When he looked back at Brayden, his brother gestured that he heard something.

Maybe someone was inside?

He eased open the door, gun at the ready, and inched inside. Brayden peeked past him. The interior was dark and appeared deserted. At one time, this place housed tourists and travelers driving from Austin toward Mexico. It had drawn miners but also catered to cattle ranchers and horse lovers.

Paintings of wild mustangs hung in the entryway,

where the wallpaper was fading, the curtains a dull pale gray.

Lucas swung left and Brayden went right. He scanned the dining room while his brother ducked into a formal living room/parlor that had probably once hosted afternoon tea for guests.

The room was empty, but led to a large kitchen with a giant oak table. A case of bottled water sat on a grimy counter. Loaves of bread, canned beans and cans of soup filled a box indicating a recent shopping trip.

Someone had been here.

A noise sounded from upstairs, and he froze. Maybe someone was still here.

Lucas's footsteps echoed from the front. He must be going up the staircase. A back stairwell caught Brayden's eye, and he headed toward it. He forced his footfalls to remain light, although the old wooden floors squeaked as he climbed them.

He stopped on the landing and noted a large room to the right. The hall led to other rooms that had once been rented to guests.

Lucas appeared at the opposite end, then ducked into one of the bedrooms. Brayden veered into the larger room, which must have been used as a suite. The front area held a love seat, chair and coffee table. He crept toward the inner door and thought he heard a noise coming from behind it.

He hesitated, listening for voices, determined not to walk into a trap. No male voices. Maybe someone crying?

His pulse jumped. Was it Izzy?

Body coiled with tension, he eased open the door, keeping his gun braced in case one of DiSanti's men lay waiting on the other side. Another sound. A moan.

Crying. Definitely crying.

Anger forced him forward, his temper rising even more when he spotted three cots in the room. Cots where three young girls lay.

In one quick glance, he realized they'd been drugged. Two of them were either asleep or unconscious while the third, a scrawny brunette who was probably about thirteen, lay huddled with her knees up, sobbing into her hands.

He took a deep breath, then slowly approached her. His foot made the floor creak, and she startled and jerked her head up, her eyes wide with terror.

"Shh, it's okay," he murmured. "I'm here to help you."

She scooted as far as possible against the wall, body trembling, eyes red and swollen from crying. He took a step closer, wanting to check the other girls' pulses, but she shrieked and shook her head wildly, causing him to stop.

He held up his hand in a sign that he wouldn't hurt them. "You're okay now. I'm going to get help."

She stared at him wide-eyed, and he backed toward the door. He ran into Lucas in the hall.

"There are three girls in there," he told his brother.

"Two more in the other room," Lucas said gruffly. "Both drugged and unconscious." He removed his phone from his pocket. "I'll call an ambulance."

Brayden nodded. "I'll get Mila."

"Good idea." Lucas walked to the door to peek in on the three girls Brayden had found, his expression grim.

They still needed to check the outbuildings, but he'd get Mila first.

MILA CHECKED HER phone a dozen times, hoping for another message, but nothing yet.

She had to do whatever DiSanti's men said. But separating herself from Brayden and Lucas would be difficult. And how would she rescue Izzy on her own?

If she went with them, they still might kill her and Izzy…

A movement on the hill startled her. Brayden exited the inn. His face looked stony as he scanned the property and exterior of the outbuildings. Then he hurried toward the woods where they'd parked.

She'd hoped he'd find Izzy, but that text had killed her hopes. If there was nothing here, maybe Brayden was ready to go. She'd have him drive her back to her place or the clinic, somewhere she'd have access to a car.

He tapped on the window, and she unlocked the door and opened it with a shaky hand.

"We found some girls inside," Brayden said. "They've been drugged. We need you."

Her medical training kicked in, and she scrambled out of the car.

"I don't have a medical bag with me," she said, frustrated. She always carried one in her car. She might need one when she found her daughter.

"It's okay. Lucas called an ambulance so help should

be here soon. One girl is conscious and terrified of me. Maybe you can calm her until the medics arrive."

"Of course." Mila raced beside him as they climbed the hill. "Any sign of DiSanti or his men?"

"Just some cans of food and water, but no evidence of DiSanti or medical supplies." His breath heaved out as they made it to the door. "No telling how long the girls have been here. This is probably a holding spot until they can move or sell them."

Lucas met them at the bottom of the stairs. "Two in the room on the end. Both have pulses, but they're weak. I was afraid to get too close to the others and spook the one who's conscious. Ambulance should be here in ten."

"No sign of Izzy?" Mila asked.

Lucas shook his head. "Perhaps the girl who's conscious can tell us something about where they were going."

Mila latched onto that hope as she followed Brayden up the stairs. The dust, cobwebs, fading wallpaper and scratched floors were a sign that the inn hadn't been used in at least a decade.

DiSanti had taken advantage of that just like he took advantage of everything else.

"Brace yourself," Brayden said in a low voice. "It's not pretty."

"I've seen a lot of bad things in my field," Mila said, although the inhumane treatment people inflicted on others never ceased to amaze—and disgust—her.

Brayden opened the door, but she motioned for him to let her enter first. The lighting was dim, the smell of sweat and urine strong. Someone had also been sick.

She breathed out, emotions welling inside her at the

sight of the two unconscious girls on the cots. Both wore dresses way too short for them, which had ridden up their legs as they lay sprawled on the beds.

The third girl was shaking and crying, her arms wrapped around her knees, her fear a palpable force in the room.

"Hi," she said in a soft tone as she slowly walked toward the teens. "My name is Dr. Mila Manchester." She offered the frightened girl a warm smile. "My friend Brayden works with the police. We're here to rescue you." The crying girl sniffed and clenched her legs tighter.

"I promise, we won't hurt you. We know some bad men brought you here, and we're going to take you to the hospital for treatment, then make sure you're safe."

The girl's face crumpled, and a wail escaped her. Mila was afraid she'd said the wrong thing, but she didn't have time to second-guess herself. No telling what DiSanti's cronies had done to the young girl.

She approached the cots where the two unconscious girls lay, hair spilled on the pillows, bodies limp. At first glance, they didn't appear to be breathing. She stooped between the two cots and gently pressed her hand to the first girl's cheek, a sandy-blonde girl with pale skin and freckles. Her skin felt cold and clammy, and she didn't respond. Mila checked for a pulse and was relieved to find one, although, as Lucas reported on the other two teens, it was weak.

She gave Brayden a quick nod to indicate the girl was alive, then turned to the other, an auburn-haired girl. Bruises darkened the pale skin beneath her eyes and covered her legs. One arm dangled from the side of the bed, while the other hand clutched the sheet to her as if she was fighting to cover herself and preserve her dignity.

Mila checked for a pulse, then breathed a sigh of relief that she had one. Gently, she stroked the girl's cold cheek with the back of her hand. "Hang in there, sweetheart. You're going to be okay."

Anger churned in her belly at what these girls had endured. They had to survive.

All the more reason to save Izzy. If not, and DiSanti killed her and kept Izzy alive, she might end up like these teenagers. That was not going to happen to her daughter, no matter what she had to do.

Satisfied the girls were breathing, she turned her attention to the brunette staring at her with terror-glazed eyes.

"Hey, sweetie, I told you my name is Dr. Manchester, but you can call me Mila."

The girl clamped her teeth over her lower lip and simply stared at her with distrust.

Who could blame her? She had reason not to trust.

Mila offered her a sympathetic smile. "Your friends, the other girls here, they're alive, and I'm going to make sure they receive medical treatment." And psychiatric help if needed.

"I understand that you're scared," Mila said, inching closer. "But everything's going to be all right. You're never going to have to see those bad men again."

The girl's breath hitched.

Mila offered her another smile. "What's your name, sweetie?"

The girl gave a wary nod, then whispered, "Keenan."

"Hi, Keenan, it's nice to meet you. Like I said, my name is Mila. I'm a doctor. Can you tell me how you ended up here?"

The girl whimpered. "They took me…from the shelter," she said in a raw whisper.

"I'm so sorry, honey." She patted the girl's thin hand. "Do you have some family I can call? A mother? Father? Grandparent?"

Keenan shook her head no. "My grandma took me to the shelter when we got evicted, but she was sick… and she didn't make it."

"Do you remember the name of the shelter?"

The girl rubbed her forehead, then shook her head. "No, it was late, and I was so upset over Granny that I didn't pay attention."

"Shh, it's all right now. I promise I'll take care of you." She reached out and patted Keenan's thin shoulder, relieved when the young girl didn't jerk away. "I think you were drugged. Am I right?"

Another nod.

"Do you have any idea what they gave you?"

Keenan shook her head no.

"Was it in your food? Or did they inject you?"

The girl held out her arm. Mila gritted her teeth at the sight of the needle marks. Fury mushroomed inside her.

The sound of a siren wailed from outside, and Brayden stepped back into the room and motioned that the ambulance had arrived.

"The paramedics are going to transport you and the other girls to the hospital," Mila said.

Fear flashed in Keenan's eyes, and she clutched Mila's hand, her ragged nails digging into Mila's palms.

Mila's heart ached for her. "I'll go with you," Mila promised. "And I'll stay with you every step of the way."

The girl nodded vigorously, tears trickling down her cheek. Fear streaked her face as she glanced at the door. "They're coming back for us," she said on a sob.

Mila glanced at Brayden, then squeezed the girl's hand. "They won't find you, I promise. Brayden's brother is with the FBI."

Brayden murmured that it would be okay, too. "We'll post someone here and catch them when they return," Brayden assured her.

Mila inhaled a deep breath. "Keenan, the men who brought you here and drugged you work for another man named DiSanti. Does that name sound familiar?"

Keenan gave a small shrug. "Maybe."

Mila patted her arm. "I need to ask you one more question." She removed her phone and showed her a picture of Izzy. "I think those same men kidnapped my little girl. She's only three and her name is Izzy."

The girl's eyes widened, and she gasped for a breath, as if she was having a panic attack.

Panic clawed at Mila. "Did you see Izzy? Was she here?"

Chapter Sixteen

Mila felt as if her heart stopped beating. "Keenan, have you seen this little girl?"

The young girl wiped at her tears with the back of a bruised hand and gave a little nod.

Mila's pulse jumped. "Was she here?"

The girl nodded again.

Mila swallowed back a sob. "Was she okay? Was she hurt?"

Keenan's look softened. "She was scared, but Jade took care of her."

"Jade?"

"She was one of us," Keenan said. "She kept the little girl close to her, and told the men to leave them alone."

Relief lightened Mila's fear for a millisecond. At least they hadn't hurt Izzy. Not yet.

But Lucas was searching the outbuildings now.

She held Keenan's hand again, warming it between her own. "When did they leave you here?"

"This morning."

Damn. If they'd only gotten here sooner...

She straightened. She had to focus. "Was Jade with Izzy when they left?"

Keenan nodded. "The little girl was clinging to her."

Emotions throbbed inside Mila's chest. "Did the men say where they were going?"

The young girl rubbed her forehead again, her eyes crinkling. "No…at least I didn't hear them."

Footsteps sounded in the hall, then Brayden appeared with two medics.

Mila patted Keenan's hand and stood. "It's going to be okay now. Hang in there, sweetie."

Mila hurried to meet the medics and watched as they began taking vitals.

"Let's get them to the hospital stat," Mila said. "I want a full blood panel to identify the drugs they were given, also rape kits and full body workups."

The next few minutes were hectic as the medics carried the teens to the ambulance. Keenan was weak, but seemed to be stronger now that she realized she could trust Mila, and insisted she could walk. Mila helped her down the steps and outside.

Lucas and Brayden met them at the ambulance.

"Nothing in the outbuildings," Lucas said.

Brayden touched her elbow. "Did the girl tell you anything?"

Mila whispered to Keenan to climb in the ambulance and assured her she'd ride with her. But first she had to talk to Brayden. "Keenan said Izzy was here. A girl named Jade was taking care of her, protecting her from DiSanti's men."

"Any idea where they went?" Brayden asked.

"I'm afraid not. But they just left this morning so maybe they haven't gotten too far," Mila said.

Brayden stepped to the back of the ambulance.

"Keenan, did you see what kind of vehicle the men were driving when they left?"

The girl shook her head. "They put us in a white van."

They'd used white vans before. So generic, dammit. "I'll ask Lucas to have their analyst check traffic cams on the highways near here."

Mila checked her phone again.

Still nothing.

Frustration knotted her stomach, but she climbed in the back of the ambulance.

She'd help Keenan and the others while Lucas searched for the van.

LUCAS CALLED A crime scene team to process the house and property, then Brayden and his brother followed the ambulances to the hospital.

The staff rushed the girls to the ER, and Lucas spoke with the doctor on call to request rape kits for the victims, although the doctor reported that Mila had already requested the exams be done. Keenan became upset at the idea, but Mila soothed her and promised to stay with her every step of the way.

The next hour dragged by as they waited on tests and for the girls to regain consciousness. Lucas checked in constantly with his people, hoping for word on the van or DiSanti.

Brayden phoned Dexter to relay the latest events.

"I've been digging into locals who might be involved in this trafficking unit. Lem Corley is on Lucas's short list," Dexter said. "Word is that he's retired and hired a cowboy out of El Paso to run the cattle ranching business. He's also bought up property near the Mexican border in Juarez."

"We know that. Do you have anything new?" Brayden asked. "What about his financials?"

"Corley has a hefty savings, but he could argue that he's built that from the cattle operation." Dexter paused. "I found an offshore account with a couple million in it. There's no indication that his business pulled in that kind of money."

Brayden chewed the inside of his cheek. "That is suspicious."

"Could be drugs," Dexter said.

"Or he could be shuffling young women across the border for DiSanti." Brayden glanced at Lucas, who was talking to one of the nurses. "Send me the address for the ranch near Austin. We'll talk to Corley once we finish here."

"Copy that. I'll keep digging and see if I can find out more on that property in Juarez."

Brayden thanked him, then hung up and joined Lucas.

"The girls are traumatized," the doctor said. "Two of them regained consciousness, but they're terrified and not talking. I've requested a psych exam and counselor."

"Let me call my wife, Charlotte," Lucas said. "You may remember her from a few months ago when her art therapy studio was invaded and four of her students were abducted."

The doctor nodded. "Yes, I was glad to hear that they were all found alive and safe."

"We think the man who orchestrated their abduction spearheaded the Shetland operation," Lucas said.

"We also believe he's behind the trafficking ring that was holding the five victims here hostage. It's imperative I speak with them when they regain consciousness. They might be able to give us a lead as to where the ringleader went."

"I understand, but as I said before, these patients are severely traumatized. They need rest, medical treatment and therapy."

"My wife, Charlotte, can help," Lucas insisted. "She's an art therapist and has experience with DiSanti's victims. These girls might feel comfortable with her and open up."

"Excellent," the doctor said. "The other girls are stable, but were heavily medicated, so it may be hours before they become lucid."

"When they do, I want Charlotte to talk to them," Lucas said. "A little girl is missing and is in the hands of the leader of the trafficking ring."

The doctor wiped perspiration from his brow. "Of course."

Lucas thanked him, then stepped aside to call Charlotte. Mila appeared at the entry to the waiting room, looking worried and exhausted.

Brayden rushed toward her. He wanted to hold her, to promise her everything would be all right.

"Keenan is finally calmer and sleeping," Mila said.

"Was she able to tell you anything else?" Brayden asked.

Mila shook her head. "I'm afraid not. Unfortunately she was pretty incoherent when the men were around."

Brayden's heart went out to the girl and to Mila. She

was a gutsy, strong woman. Even though she was terrified for her daughter, she had compassion for these victims.

"The doctor said two of the girls have regained consciousness. Maybe they can help."

Mila's eyes darkened with concern. "I hope so."

Brayden couldn't resist. He pulled her up against him and wrapped his arms around her. "It's going to be okay, Mila. We'll find her."

Her heavy breathing punctuated the air. He thought she might pull away, but she laid her head against his chest and seemed to give in to her own needs for a moment. He rubbed her back, rocking her gently in his arms. When she lifted her head and looked into his eyes, the agony in hers nearly sent him to his knees.

"Keenan is so lost," Mila said. "I don't know if she'll ever truly recover. Or the others."

He offered a smile of encouragement. "It may seem like that now, but I've seen the progress Charlotte's students have made these last few months. It's amazing. With her help and my mother's love, they feel secure now and are moving on, even looking forward to the future. They have a family, even if it's not the one they were born to."

Mila bit down on her lip, then pulled away.

"Did I say something wrong? You don't think that my mother could love them like they're her own?"

Mila stiffened. "Of course I believe that. I was adopted myself." She thumbed a strand of hair away from her cheek. "You said two of the girls are awake now. I'd like to talk to them."

"I know. So would I, but the doctor asked us to wait.

Lucas is calling Charlotte to come and counsel the girls. Maybe you and Charlotte can talk with them together."

Mila nodded. "Yes, I'm sure they need a counselor after what they've been through. And I promise not to push them too hard. I want what's best for the girls, too."

She was the most unselfish woman Brayden had ever met. He was falling for her.

That thought should have shaken him up.

But for some reason, in the midst of the ugliness surrounding him, it felt right.

"Charlotte is on her way." Lucas's commanding voice forced Brayden to put his personal thoughts on hold. He jerked his mind back to the case.

"Dexter sent me GPS coordinates for Lem Corley's ranch. He checked Corley's financials and found an off shore account with a hefty amount in it. He's also looking into his property in Juarez."

"It's near the border," Lucas said. "We have an agent investigating it."

"He could be helping DiSanti move victims across the border into Mexico."

A muscle ticked in Lucas's jaw. "I'm going to talk to him now."

Brayden cleared his throat. "I'll go with you." He glanced at Mila. "That is, if you'll be okay here for a while."

Mila clasped her hands together. "I'll be fine. I want to stay with the girls until they're out of the woods."

MILA MEANT WHAT she'd told Brayden. But even as she'd assured Keenan she was safe, all she could think about was Izzy and what was happening to her.

If DiSanti could possibly have figured out that she was his child.

She prayed not, that her secret was safe.

She'd die before she'd let that bastard know he had a precious little girl. Izzy belonged to her.

She went to the vending machines, bought a cup of coffee and carried it back to the waiting room. Charlotte was just coming in the door when she arrived. She made a beeline toward Mila, then embraced her.

They were both a little teary when they pulled away.

"Lucas said that one of the girls saw Izzy. That's good news, Mila."

Mila forced a smile, although her heart wasn't in it. "That's been hours though." It had been hours since that text message too and still no word of what she should do.

DiSanti wanted her to lose the feds. Did that mean he was watching her to see if she complied?

She glanced around the hospital, suddenly suspicious that one of the staff or maybe one of the people in the waiting room—there was a big guy in a hoodie—might be on DiSanti's payroll. He could have planted someone to follow her.

The doctor on call, a man named Dr. Hembry, approached her. "Dr. Manchester, I came to give you an update. The two girls who regained consciousness are physically going to be fine. But they're scared to death."

Mila gestured toward Charlotte. "This is Charlotte Reacher Hawk, the wife of the federal agent you were talking to. He told you she could help."

"That's right, you're the therapist." He shook Charlotte's hand. "At this point, having a kind face, especially a woman's, will go a long way."

"Then I can see them?" Charlotte asked.

Dr. Hembry nodded. "We thought it might help if we put the girls in the same room," Dr. Hembry said.

He led the two of them to an ER room, and they slipped inside.

Mila took one look at the two young girls, and hated DiSanti more than ever. The battered teens looked lost and terrified and small in the hospital beds.

She and Charlotte approached slowly, and Mila explained that she was with the federal agent who'd rescued them.

Charlotte introduced herself, then Mila did the same.

She offered them a sympathetic smile. "I understand you've both been through a frightening ordeal, and we want to help you."

Charlotte scooted a chair between the beds, so she could face both girls. "I'm here for whatever you need," she said softly. "I know some other girls who were abducted by the same man who took you. We rescued them last year, and they're safe now. So are you."

The girls traded wary looks, both limp from the drugs and their ordeal.

"You can start by telling us your names," Charlotte said. "Also, tell us if you have family or a friend that you want us to call."

Unfortunately, the girls had no one to call just as Keenan hadn't. Perfect targets for DiSanti's people.

She and Charlotte spent the next hour soothing the girls and coaxing them to open up. Anita Robinson was fourteen, from El Paso and had run away from home after her mother died. Left with a stepfather who abused her, she took to the streets. She had no idea how long she'd been held hostage and had no family to call. But she'd ended up at a group home called Happy Trails.

Frannie Fenter was thirteen. She was kidnapped outside the group home where she was living. The same group home, Happy Trails, a ranch that supposedly helped orphans as the Hawks were doing.

Was the home legit or part of the Shetland operation?

IZZY CURLED UP with the raggedy blanket the big girl had given her. She was cold, hungry and scared. She wanted her mommy bad.

Tears ran down her face, but she pressed her fist to her mouth so she wouldn't cry out loud.

Jade, the girl who'd let her sleep with her the night before, rubbed her arm and shushed her.

She tried not to cry. But she couldn't help it. She wanted her mommy. She missed her and Roberta and Brownie and her pretty bed with the pink quilt. She wanted to run and play in her backyard and dig up worms and climb on her jungle gym. There were bird's eggs in a nest, too. Had the babies hatched already?

"I wanna go home," she whimpered. "I want Mama."

Jade wrapped the blanket around her tighter and pulled her up against her. "I know, sweetie. I know."

Jade looked sad, too. She said she hadn't seen her mother in years.

That made Izzy even more scared that she'd never see her mama again.

Chapter Seventeen

Mila stewed over what the girls had revealed so far. None of them had families, making them easy targets for DiSanti's men. Without family to report them missing, it might take months before anyone realized they were gone.

Except the head of the group home would have known.

Mila wanted to know more, but first, she had to ask them about her daughter. She showed them Izzy's photo. "This is my little girl. She's only three. Keenan said that she was at the house where you were. Do either of you recall seeing her?"

Frannie nodded, but Anita shook her head.

"I'm sorry. I don't remember much," Anita said.

"Did the men say anything about where they were going when they left?" Mila asked.

Frannie's lower lip quivered. "I heard one of them say they had to move us again, but they needed to take care of something first."

"Do you know what that something was?" Mila asked.

She shook her head. "It seemed important though. He shouted at the other man."

Charlotte stroked Frannie's arm. "You're doing great, sweetie. Did he mention a name? Or a place?"

Frannie's face paled. "I'm sorry. I wish I could help, but…he saw me watching, and gave me more drugs."

"Did they mention where they were taking Izzy?" Mila asked. "A town or another state? Or out of the country?"

"I…don't know…" Frannie grew agitated, and Anita wiped at more tears. Mila knew she was pushing hard, but her daughter's life was at stake.

"Tell us about the group home where you were living," Mila said gently.

"It was called Happy Trails," Frannie said. "We were supposed to work with the horses and learn to ride. But it didn't turn out that way at all."

"What happened?" Charlotte asked.

She cast her eyes downward, fear flashing across her face.

"Listen to me," Charlotte said in a tender but firm voice. "You're not in trouble, and you haven't done anything wrong."

"She's right," Mila said softly.

Charlotte cleared her throat. "You can tell us anything, no matter how bad you think it might sound, and we promise not to judge. We're here to help, and will do whatever necessary to make sure you're safe."

Frannie and Anita exchanged looks, then Frannie cleared her throat. "It wasn't a horse ranch at all. At first, they made us do chores and work outside on the farm. But then…"

Mila's stomach knotted. "Then what?"

"They brought men in," Anita cried. "They made us

dress up in skimpy party dresses, then took pictures of us. I think they put them on the internet."

Mila forced herself not to react, but she was seething inside. DiSanti's men would use the photos as advertisements to sell the girls to the highest bidder.

"YOU TOLD HARRISON where we're going?" Brayden asked Lucas as they drove to Corley's ranch.

"Yeah. I would have asked him to meet us, but Corley's ranch is out of his jurisdiction. Harrison assigned a couple of deputies to watch Hawk's Landing in case DiSanti's men traced Mila there."

"Good. We want Mom and the other girls safe." Brayden paused. "And Honey, too. That baby means everything to Harrison."

"He is excited about being a daddy," Lucas said with a twitch to his mouth.

"How about you and Charlotte? Any talk of kids?"

Lucas cut his eyes sideways. "She went through a lot this last year. We're taking our time, but maybe soon."

Envy stirred inside Brayden.

"Has Mila said anything else about Izzy's father?" Lucas asked.

Brayden clenched his jaw. He hadn't exactly pushed her for information the way Lucas had suggested. "I told you he's dead, so I don't see how he'd have anything to do with this."

Lucas veered down the long drive to the Corley ranch, which consisted of acres and acres of pastures for his cattle. The barns and stables looked weathered as if they were in disrepair. Odd since his financials indicated that he had money to invest back into the place.

Late-afternoon shadows darkened the tree-lined drive. A couple of pickup trucks were parked by one of the outbuildings.

Lucas barreled over the ruts in the road and came to a stop at a farmhouse that looked as if it had been built a hundred years ago.

"He sure as hell hasn't put his money into fixing up his place," Brayden commented.

"I spoke to the deputy director earlier. He sent two agents to investigate Corley's property near Juarez."

Brayden's stomach tightened. "We can't let DiSanti's men take Izzy across the border."

"I've alerted the border patrol along with the airports and train stations to be on the lookout for Izzy," Lucas said.

Brayden had mixed feelings about that. He wanted a damn Amber Alert issued across the country. But doing so might spook DiSanti into carrying out his threats.

He couldn't live with that.

"I requested a warrant for Corley's computers, finances and electronic transmissions," Lucas said as he parked. "But the judge denied it. Said we didn't have probable cause."

Brayden silently cursed, Sometimes the law worked for them and sometimes against them. The reason Dexter did things his way.

"A missing child sounds like probable cause to me."

"I'm still working on it. Our analyst is looking for connections." Lucas checked his gun, then opened his car door and slid out. Brayden followed, his gaze scanning the property for signs of trouble. No gunmen in sight.

That didn't mean they weren't hiding in the shadows though.

He and Lucas walked up the graveled drive to the sagging porch and climbed the steps. A beagle lay snoring near a rusted porch swing.

Lucas knocked, and a minute later, a short robust woman wearing an apron answered the door. Lucas flashed his ID and introduced them, then asked her name.

"Harriet," she said.

"Have you worked here long?" Lucas asked.

"A few months," Harriet said. "I do the cooking and cleaning for the hands."

"We need to speak to Lem Corley," Lucas said. "Is he here?"

She gestured for them to come in. "In the back. He was just about to head back out. I'll go get him."

"Wait," Lucas said. "Can we ask you something first?"

A wary look crossed her face, and she wiped her hands on her apron. "I suppose. What's going on?"

Lucas showed her a picture of Izzy. "We're looking for this little girl. She's missing."

She narrowed her eyes as she studied the picture. "Haven't seen a child around this place, not since I've been here." She looked back up at Lucas. "What makes you think she'd be here?"

Lucas removed another photo from his pocket. DiSanti. "This man is wanted for human trafficking. We believe he and his men kidnapped the little girl. Have you seen him before?"

"I don't believe so. It's pretty quiet around here.

Mostly the ranch hands. Occasionally Mr. Corley has one of his friends from the Cattleman's club out to talk business, but they hole up in his study so I don't really know any of them." She folded her arms across her ample stomach. "Why would you think Mr. Corley knows this man?"

Lucas maintained a poker face. "We're talking to anyone who owns large plots of land where DiSanti's men could hide the girls they abduct before trafficking them to buyers. Corley has property here and near Juarez, so his name cropped up."

She looked relieved. "I see. Well, I've never been to his Juarez place, but I can tell you that I haven't seen or heard of any girls being brought here."

Dammit. The property was large enough for the men to hide away from the house. But he and Lucas needed a warrant to search the land.

"What in the hell are you telling my cook?" a man's deep voice bellowed.

Harriet startled and pressed one hand over her mouth as Corley stomped toward her.

"Harriet?"

"I'm sorry, Mr. Corley," Harriet said. "These men are looking for a missing child, and were just asking some questions."

Corley pushed past her and confronted them, eyes blazing with anger. "I don't know why in the hell you'd think I'd know anything about a missing kid. I run cattle here."

"We're aware of that," Lucas said. "But you have a big spread, and it's possible that the men who abducted her could be hiding out on your property without your knowledge."

Corley scrubbed a hand over his balding head. He looked confused by Lucas's statement. Brayden admired his brother's tactic.

"The men who kidnapped her are extremely dangerous, Mr. Corley," Lucas said. "You wouldn't want to endanger your hands or Harriet, would you?"

"Uh...of course not," Corley stammered.

"Then you won't mind showing us around your property," Lucas said, his voice calm, nonjudgmental.

Corley shifted. "Do you have a warrant?"

Lucas's brow lifted in a challenge. "If you don't have anything to hide, then why would I need one?"

Corley inched backward as if to argue, but then seemed to think better of it. "All right. I'll show you around, then you can get off my property and leave me alone."

"Thanks for your cooperation," Lucas said.

Brayden followed them outside to Corley's truck.

Lucas gestured toward the vehicle. "It's a tight fit. Why don't you wait here, Brayden?"

Brayden jammed his hands in the pockets of his jacket and watched Corley and Lucas drive away.

Lucas had just given him a chance to dig around. He'd talk to Harriet again, then slip out to the stables and barn and talk to Corley's hands without Corley breathing down his neck.

MILA PATTED FRANNIE'S HAND. "Can you tell us how to get to Happy Trails?"

The girl shrugged. "Not really. The social worker from the shelter drove us there."

"From the shelter?" Mila asked.

Frannie nodded. "That's where I met Keenan."

Keenan had mentioned a shelter where her grandmother had taken her.

"What was the name of this social worker?" Charlotte asked.

Anita piped up. "Valeria. She was nice until she took us to that ranch. When I told her I didn't want to stay, she got mad and said I had no place to go, that I had to earn my keep."

"She told me the same thing," Frannie said.

Mila gritted her teeth. "Do you remember Valeria's last name?"

Both girls shook their heads.

"How about an agency she worked with?"

Again, neither knew the answer to that question. Which meant she might not have worked with an agency at all.

"Maybe Lucas can find out her name," Charlotte said.

"We need to locate this place, Happy Trails," Mila said. "Izzy might be there."

Charlotte clenched her hand. "We'll let Lucas and Brayden know. If she's there, they'll get her back."

Charlotte's trust and confidence in the Hawk men was rubbing off on Mila. She couldn't give up.

Her daughter needed her.

Charlotte retrieved her sketch pad. "Girls, let's see

if you can describe the social worker who dropped you at Happy Trails."

"We'll try," Frannie said.

Anita spoke up. "She was tall, thin and had dark hair pulled back in a tight bun."

Charlotte quickly drew the image.

"Her features were sharp," Frannie said. "She had high cheekbones. Plump lips. And thick eyebrows."

Charlotte finished detailing the features.

"Was there anyone else with you at the ranch?" Mila asked.

Anita glanced down at her bruised knuckles. "Another lady. She was older, and she seemed afraid of the men."

"What was her name?" Mila asked.

"They called her Shanika," Frannie said.

Charlotte settled her sketch pad on her lap and removed her pencils.

Mila gripped her phone in her hand. "I'm going to call Brayden and tell him what we learned."

Charlotte nodded, and Mila left the room.

Her pulse hammered as she checked her phone for messages. Still no word about what DiSanti wanted her to do.

BRAYDEN GAVE HARRIET his business card. "This little girl's life is in danger. If you hear something that can help, please call me." He touched her arm gently. "I'm a lawyer. I can protect you."

She gave him a wary look, but nodded that she would. Brayden walked out to the barn and approached one of the hands, a tall dark-haired Hispanic cowboy. He was cleaning one of the stalls.

The cowboy jerked his head up at the sight of Brayden, then started to run. Brayden jogged after him and snatched him before he could exit the barn. He jerked the man around to face him and pushed him against the stall.

"You know the reason I'm here?" Brayden asked.

The man frowned. "I…heard you with Mr. Corley."

"What's your name?"

The man's gaze darted sideways.

"I'm not playing around here," Brayden said in a low growl. "What is your name?"

"Jorge."

Brayden clenched Jorge by the collar. "Is Corley working with DiSanti, helping traffic women and girls?"

The man shrugged. "I don't know anything about it. I'm just supposed to clean stalls and repair fences."

"Tell me what you do know," Brayden said.

"I told you I don't know anything." Fear vibrated in Jorge's voice.

Brayden arched his brows. "Then why run?"

Jorge lowered his gaze toward the ground, and the truth hit Brayden. "Because you're in the country illegally, aren't you?"

Shame and fear darted into the man's eyes as he glanced up at Brayden. "He said he knew somebody. That I could earn my freedom."

Anger radiated through Brayden. So Corley, or Di-

Santi, or both, had used Jorge's status as an immigrant to coerce him into doing their dirty work.

His gaze met Jorge's. "Just what did you have to do to earn it?"

Chapter Eighteen

Indecision played across the ranch hand's face. Jorge was definitely scared. Of being deported? Or maybe his family had been threatened as Mila's had?

The sound of an engine roaring closer made panic streak Jorge's face. Corley and Lucas returning. Dammit.

"I told you I know nothing," the cowboy said. "I just do my job."

"Does that job entail holding innocent girls hostage?"

A muscle ticked in the young man's jaw as he looked down at his shovel.

"We think that's what Corley is into," Brayden said. "Do you really want to live off money made that way? Is your freedom worth the life of a little three-year-old girl?"

Jorge winced.

"Think about it," Brayden said as Corley approached. "Do you have a sister or friend with a sister? Would you want her sold as a sex slave?"

The man looked up at him as if he was going to say

something, but Corley's truck roared to a stop in front of them, gravel spewing, and Jorge clammed up.

Brayden slipped a business card from his pocket and pushed it into Jorge's hand. "Call me if you can help. If they take this little girl out of the country, her mother may never see her again."

The truck door slammed, and Corley climbed out, looking pissed. Lucas followed, his expression indicating he hadn't found anything helpful.

Brayden's cell phone buzzed. Mila.

He quickly connected. "Yeah?"

"Did you find her?" Mila asked, her voice quivering.

God, he hated to tell her no. "Not at Corley's. Hopefully one of the ranch hands or the cook will talk. We'll see."

A tense heartbeat passed. "Charlotte and I have been talking to the girls who regained consciousness. They're frightened, but they said that they were taken from a group home called Happy Trails. It was supposed to be a ranch for girls, but men were brought there for them to entertain. They were also dressed up and photographed."

"For potential clients," Brayden guessed.

"I think so."

"Where is this place?" Brayden asked.

"Neither girl knew the location. I was hoping you could find out."

"I'll talk to Lucas. Anything else?"

"A social worker named Valeria took them to the home. She might be in on the Shetland operation."

Hard to believe another woman would be involved, but it happened.

"A woman named Shanika was also at the ranch," Mila said. "Izzy could be there, Brayden."

"Lucas and I will get right on it. Hang in there."

"I could go with you," Mila said.

Brayden hesitated. If Happy Trails was a holding ground for the Shetland operation, it would be dangerous.

"I think you're better off there," Brayden said. "You and Charlotte did good today. See what else you can learn from the victims."

Silence stretched between them for a long moment. "Mila?"

"I'm here," she said. "Just find her, Brayden. I can't let her end up like these girls."

He wouldn't let that happen either. "I promise, we'll bring her back to you."

Damn, even as he made the promise, he knew he shouldn't, that he might not be able to deliver on it.

Then Mila would hate him.

That bothered him more than he wanted to admit.

He wanted to be her hero. Save her daughter.

Be the man she could turn to and trust.

Disappointing her would crush him.

THE AFTERNOON DRAGGED into evening as Mila and Charlotte sat with the girls. They moved Keenan in with Frannie and Anita and encouraged them to rest.

Mila checked her phone a dozen times, but still no word. She paced the waiting room while Charlotte went to check on the other two girls.

Why had DiSanti's men sent her that message and not followed through?

Her anxiety rose with every passing second. Did they know she'd turned to the Hawks for help? Had they discovered that Lucas and Brayden had rescued these girls?

Would they punish her daughter because they'd foiled DiSanti's plans?

Charlotte appeared with coffee in hand. "Unfortunately, the other girls couldn't offer anything more. Except that one of them confirmed that a girl named Jade was with Izzy and that she was taking care of her."

That was a small relief, but Mila latched onto it as they walked back to say good-night to the girls.

Lucas had arranged for guards to watch the girls' rooms, and the doctor agreed to keep her updated. Charlotte planned to coordinate with the Department of Family and Protective Services regarding the teens.

Charlotte hugged each of them and promised to visit the next day.

"What's going to happen to us?" Keenan asked.

Charlotte stroked Keenan's hand. "We'll find you a safe place to live, someone who'll care for you and help you get back on your feet, and back in school. Everything's going to be all right."

Mila hugged her, as well. "She's right, Keenan. Charlotte and I are on your side. You're not alone now."

Keenan didn't look completely convinced, but her eyes were closing, fatigue weighing on her, and she drifted to sleep.

"Come on," Charlotte said. "Ava has dinner waiting for us."

"Ava?"

"Lucas's mother," Charlotte said. "She's amazing. Honey and Harrison will be there, too."

Mila hesitated, willing a message to appear on her phone. But she checked it. Nothing.

"I don't want to endanger the Hawks," Mila said.

Charlotte grabbed her hand. "We all have a vested interest in seeing that DiSanti is stopped once and for all. You'll understand when you meet the girls the Hawks took in." A twinkle flickered in Charlotte's eye. "Besides, we have to talk to Ava and see if she has room in her heart for a few more young women in need."

It took a while to locate Happy Trails. Brayden would have thought it would have been well-known, at least on the internet, but it wasn't.

A sign of what it had been used for and by whom. DiSanti's group had wanted to keep it under the radar.

Damn him.

Charlotte had faxed sketches of Valeria and Shanika to Lucas to forward to the FBI field office in Austin. Their analyst forwarded them to law enforcement agencies and alerted airports, train and bus stations, and the border patrol to be on the lookout for the women, especially if they were traveling with a little girl.

Izzy had been gone too damn long for comfort. For all they knew, DiSanti's people could have carried her halfway across the world by now.

Or killed her and dumped her little body someplace where they might never find her.

No. He couldn't let himself think about the worst case. And he certainly couldn't divulge those concerns to Mila.

He and his family understood how painful it was to

live year after year with no word of where your loved one was, or if they were dead or alive.

First his little sister, Chrissy. Then his father.

Lucas's phone buzzed, and he hit Connect. "Yeah. Okay. See you there."

"That was Charlotte," he said when he hung up. "She's driving Mila to the ranch. Mom has dinner. I told her we'd meet them there."

Brayden nodded. His mother would love Mila.

He liked her. A lot. Maybe more than like. He wanted to be with her and rescue her daughter more than he'd ever wanted anything in his life.

Lucas steered the vehicle down the road leading to Happy Trails. Brayden spotted smoke in the distance.

"Look," he said, pointing toward the east. "There's a fire."

Lucas hit the gas and sped up. "That's the ranch," he said through gritted teeth.

Brayden gripped the seat edge as Lucas raced toward the smoke. Gravel spewed from their tires, gears grinding as he maneuvered a pothole and flew over a small hill. The smoke was growing thicker, curling up into the sky.

As soon as they dipped downhill, Brayden spotted flames. They engulfed the main house and two buildings to the side.

"Call the fire department," Lucas said as he took the curve on two wheels.

Brayden punched 9-1-1 and gripped the seat edge as Lucas swung the vehicle near a cluster of live oaks and careened to a stop. Flames shot into the sky, lighting up the darkness. Suddenly a black pickup darted from behind the burning building and roared past them.

Brayden threw the car door open and jumped out. "Go after him! I'll see if anyone's inside!"

Lucas hesitated for a second, but Brayden waved at him to go. If the person in the car knew where Izzy was, he was getting away.

Lucas sped after the vehicle, and Brayden ran toward the burning farmhouse. Flames shot from the roof and back of the house, and smoke billowed upward in a thick fog.

Brayden yanked a bandanna from inside his jacket and tied it around his mouth, then darted through the front door. Smoke seeped through the entry, but the blaze hadn't yet reached the doorway.

He conducted a quick survey of the house. All one floor. Rooms to the right, a hall to the left that probably led to bedrooms.

"Is anyone here?" he shouted as he glanced down the hall.

Wood crackled and popped in the blaze, but he didn't hear voices. Still, he shouted again and again as he raced down the hall to the bedrooms. He jumped over wood that had splintered down from the ceiling, dodging flames as the fire crawled along the doorways eating the rotting wood.

Two rooms held a series of single beds that resembled a dorm. He counted a dozen, although fire was spreading quickly. He dodged flames as he checked the closets to make sure no one was hiding or had been left inside.

Flames rippled up the wall, catching the curtains on fire and crawling toward the beds. He raced to the next room, dodging falling debris, and wove between patches of burning embers to check those beds and the closet. Clothes inside the closet were aflame, but no one was inside.

Relieved, he headed back to the front then into the hall toward the kitchen. Already fire blazed a trail along the back wall. He coughed, but had to check the storage closet.

Smoke created a thick fog, but he dived through it, calling out as he went. Surely DiSanti's goonies wouldn't have left anyone inside, especially Izzy.

He reached out to touch the doorknob of the pantry, but it was hot, so he searched the kitchen for some cloths, grabbed one, wrapped it around his hand and opened the door.

His gut tightened at the sight of a woman inside the closet. Dammit. Too late. She was dead. A gunshot wound to the front of her head.

He stooped to check for a pulse anyway, but knew she was gone. Judging from the sketch Charlotte had sent, this was Shanika, the woman from Happy Trails.

THE HOMEY SCENTS of apple pie and beef stew wafted through the Hawks' main house, stirring memories of Mila's own family when she was little. Granted, they hadn't stayed in one place long, but they had shared meals as often as possible.

Mrs. Hawk took her hands and pulled her into the kitchen. "I'm so sorry for what you're going through, dear, but my boys will find your daughter. I have faith."

She wanted to have faith, too, but she was struggling. "Thank you for having me here tonight, Mrs. Hawk."

"Please call me Ava," the woman said. "We're all family."

Four teenagers were chatting and laughing as they set the table. Charlotte pulled her toward the doorway. "Mila, this is Mae Lynn, Evie, Adrian and Agnes."

The girls piped up with hellos and how much they loved the ranch.

Mila's adopted mother would have loved Ava. She'd opened her home to four teenagers in need and treated them like her own children.

The girls helped carry platters of food to the table, then the door opened and Ava greeted her oldest son, Harrison. Amazing how much the men resembled one another, but each was distinct.

"I'm Honey," a perky, very pregnant blonde said as she gave Ava a hug.

Mila exchanged greetings with the couple, her heart squeezing at the sight of Honey's blossoming belly. She hadn't gotten to carry Izzy herself, but she loved that child as if she had.

"My grandson will be here soon," Ava said with a beaming smile for Honey. "It'll be pure joy to have a baby around the house again."

Izzy's little face taunted Mila. Her arms felt empty, and she ached to hug her daughter. Never again would she take it for granted when she sang Izzy a lullaby or tucked her in bed or read her a good-night story, even if she read the same story a dozen times.

She barely managed to keep her emotions at bay during the meal. Thankfully the girls filled the silence with talk of Christmas shopping and the gifts they were making for the children's hospital. Ava was teaching them to piece quilts, and they were making blankets for the kids to snuggle with and take home when they were released.

After dessert, the teenagers retreated to the arts and craft room Ava had set up for them to work on the Christmas projects.

Harrison cleared his throat and stood. "Mom, thanks for dinner. I'm going to get Honey home. The baby's been keeping her up at night."

"It's only the beginning," Ava said with a laugh.

Mila watched as Harrison helped Honey stand. He was sweet and protective and loving just as Lucas was to Charlotte.

"I hope everything goes well during delivery," Mila said.

Honey gave Mila a sympathetic smile. "Thanks. I can't imagine what you're going through. I'll say a prayer that Lucas and Brayden find your daughter soon."

Mila thanked her, then they said good-night. "You have a beautiful family, Ava," Mila told Brayden's mother.

"I'm blessed, for sure," Ava said. "My boys, and now their wives, and now Mae Lynn and Evie and Adrian and Agnes." She pressed her hand over her chest. "My heart is bursting with love."

"I'm so proud of those girls," Charlotte said. "You've made such a difference in their lives, Ava. They're blossoming under your care."

A broad smile curved Ava Hawk's face. "They've given me just as much as I've given them." She clasped

Charlotte's hand. "Tell me about the ones you rescued today."

Mila listened quietly while Charlotte filled her in. But worry and fatigue weighed on her, and finally she stood. "If it's all right, I'm going to the cabin to get some rest." Maybe if she was alone for a while, DiSanti would finally get back in touch.

Concern darkened Charlotte's eyes. "I'll drive you over."

She didn't have time to respond. Footsteps sounded from the front. Then Lucas's and Brayden's voices.

Mila hurried to meet them, hoping they had good news. But the moment she saw their grim expressions and smelled the smoke on Brayden, her hopes died.

Charlotte and Ava joined them, and Ava gasped when she saw Brayden's soot-streaked face. "Son, what happened? Are you all right?"

"I'm fine," Brayden said. "When we reached the house at Happy Trails, it was on fire. I ran in to make sure no one was inside."

Lucas relayed how he'd chased the man who'd set the fire. "I tried to catch him, but he crashed into a ravine and died instantly."

Brayden gave Mila's arm a soft squeeze. "Izzy wasn't in the house or outbuildings, Mila. I searched every nook and corner." He sighed. "Unfortunately, we found that woman Shanika."

"Did she tell you anything?" Mila asked.

Brayden's eyes darkened. "I'm afraid not. She was dead."

Fear clogged Mila's throat, despair threatening.

DiSanti's men killed the woman who'd helped them at Happy Trails.

What did that mean for Izzy?

Chapter Nineteen

Brayden sensed despair in Mila's body language.

She had been taking care of DiSanti's victims, he reminded himself. That alone would weigh on anyone with a heart. And Mila had plenty of heart.

"Would you like to go back to the cabin?" he asked.

Mila nodded and looked down at the floor. "You're probably hungry though. Your mother made a delicious dinner."

"I'll pack him a plate to go," Ava said.

"Thanks, Mom, but Lucas and I grabbed something earlier."

Hugs went all the way around as Lucas gathered Charlotte, and he escorted Mila out to his SUV.

"Did you really eat?" Mila asked as Brayden drove her back to his cabin.

"We grabbed a burger while we were waiting on the location of Happy Trails."

He parked in front of the cabin and they went inside. "Do you mind if I take a shower?" Mila asked.

A shower was nothing. He wished he could offer her more. "Of course not. It's been a long day."

"The longest," she said in a weary voice.

He swallowed hard as he watched her duck into his guest bedroom, then the shower kicked on, and he decided to clean up himself. He smelled like smoke and soot and sweat.

The hot water felt heavenly, although thoughts of Mila in his other bathroom naked and wet ignited a different kind of tension, one that made his body harden with desire.

Dammit, Brayden. The last thing Mila needs is you coming on to her.

He toweled off, shrugged on clean jeans and a T-shirt and strode into the den. But the sound of Mila crying echoed from the bedroom and tied him in knots.

He moved to the door, his heart aching as he listened to her sob. He wanted to go to her, pull her into his arms, comfort her, assuage the agony she was feeling.

He ordered himself to walk away instead.

But her crying grew louder, and he lost his restraint. He pushed open the door and slipped inside. She stood at the window, her hair damp, her body trembling.

He closed his arms around her and pulled her against him, then held her tight.

MILA SANK AGAINST BRAYDEN, soaking in his warmth and strength. His arms felt like a safe haven, one she desperately needed at the moment.

Images of Izzy, terrified and crying for her, bombarded her, making her feel weak and helpless, chiseling away at her hope.

Brayden murmured soft, comforting words, his calm, gruff voice full of understanding.

She purged her emotions until she was exhausted

with the tears. God, she'd never been a crier, had always been tough and took charge of things like her mother.

Struggling for control, she wiped at the moisture on her cheek, then lifted her head and looked into Brayden's eyes. She expected pity, but saw compassion.

She ordered herself to pull away. But she wanted so much more.

Selfish as it was, for just a brief moment, she wanted to feel his lips against hers. Anything to drive away the pain and worry.

His eyes flickered with something dark. Sexy.

A passion that lay beneath.

His chest rose and fell against hers, and she stroked her hand over it, absorbing the solid strength in his embrace. He thumbed a strand of hair from her cheek, then heaved a breath and started to pull away.

She caught his arm and drew him back to her. Their gazes locked, heat flaring between them. He'd run into a flaming building tonight to search for her daughter, had risked his life.

Brayden Hawk was honorable and caring and a damn good man, just like his brothers. The Hawks were the most loving family she'd ever known.

Hunger blossomed inside her, and she lifted her hand and placed it against Brayden's cheek. He sucked in a harsh breath.

"Mila, you should go to bed," he said in a gruff voice.

The need in that voice and in his eyes mirrored her own. She couldn't resist. She rose on her tiptoes and pressed her lips to his, melding their mouths in a sensual kiss.

Sex appeal oozed in his touch. He was a cowboy—rugged, tough, a fighter. A man who loved the land.

He ran his hands up her back and tangled them in her hair, moving his lips across hers. First gently. Then desire spiraled, and he deepened the kiss.

She welcomed his tongue and teased him with her own.

Passion spiked inside her, and she moaned, then pushed at his T-shirt, desperate to feel his hot, bare skin against hers.

Suddenly he wrenched away. His breathing was erratic, his eyes hot with passion. "Mila, we can't." He rubbed her arms. "I don't want to take advantage of you."

He spun away from her, then walked outside onto his deck.

Tears of humiliation burned the backs of her eyelids, then she realized what he'd said. Not that he didn't want her.

He didn't want to take advantage of her.

Even in the face of her throwing herself at him, Brayden Hawk was doing the honorable thing.

His honorable intentions made her want him even more.

She inhaled a deep breath, then joined him on the deck. "It's not taking advantage of me if I want it."

BRAYDEN'S HEART POUNDED. More than anything he wanted to turn around, drag Mila into his arms, carry her to bed and make love to her.

But he forced himself to remain still. If he looked

out at the ranch long enough maybe he'd forget the desire he'd seen in her eyes.

He'd tried to do the right thing. He cared too much about Mila to hurt her or take advantage of the moment.

But it was damn hard to deny that he wanted her.

"You're vulnerable now," he said, forcing out the words. "What kind of man would I be to ignore that?"

Her footsteps sounded behind him, then she eased around to face him. Anger flared in her expressive eyes. "Either you're trying to be chivalrous, which isn't necessary since I'm a grown woman and can make decisions for myself, or you really just don't want me."

He released a pent-up breath. Then he made the mistake of looking into her eyes. Raw need darkened the depths, triggering his own hunger to override his reservations.

She parted her lips, then traced her finger over his lips, and resistance fled.

"You're sure?" he growled as he yanked her to him.

A seductive smile tilted her mouth, and he kissed her again, this time with all the need he'd tried so hard to squash earlier.

She slid her arms around his neck, and teased him with her tongue again, driving him mad with hunger. Taking her cue, he traced her lips with his own tongue, then delved inside.

She tasted like sweetness and desire and raw need all at the same time. Her hands pushed at his T-shirt, and cool air brushed his belly. Realizing they were still outside, he broke the kiss long enough to coax her inside, then swept her into another embrace.

Their hands grew frantic, pushing and tearing at each

other's clothes. Lips and tongues melded and danced in a sensual rhythm that ignited a burning fire in his belly. He wanted her naked, her skin sliding against his.

He wanted her in his bed.

She shoved his T-shirt over his head and tossed it onto the couch, and he grabbed her hand and tugged her to his bedroom. She pulled at his belt, and he ripped it off, then slowed her by slipping a finger beneath the hem of her shirt.

She made a soft sound in her throat, then removed her shirt and threw it to the floor. Heat darkened her expression as he gazed at her beautiful breasts spilling over tiny scraps of black lace.

Black lace—just as he'd fantasized.

Her lustrous hair dangled over bare shoulders, inviting his touch, and he threaded his fingers through the silky strands and yanked her to him once more. She moaned as he kissed her again, then raked his tongue and teeth along her ear and down her throat.

He backed her to the bed, and they fell on it in a tangle of arms and legs and frenzied passion. Her jeans came next, then his. He groaned at the sight of that thin strip of lace covering her femininity.

Another deep kiss, then he trailed his mouth down her throat again to her breasts. He tugged the lace aside with his teeth, then closed his mouth over one turgid nipple. She moaned and moved against him, drawing him into the V of her thighs. His sex hardened, his body pulsing with sensations as he stroked her heat with his erection.

He teased one breast, then the other, suckling her until her body quivered against him, then he dipped lower to lick and kiss her belly. His fingers toyed with the edge of her panties, his mouth watering for a taste.

She threw her head back in abandon, offering herself, and he tugged her panties off, parted her legs and dived into her honeyed sweetness with his tongue.

Passion overcame him as she fisted her hands into his hair, and he teased and tormented her with his tongue until she cried out in pleasure with her orgasm.

A SHIVER RIPPLED through Mila as erotic sensations engulfed her. Her body tingled all over, the connection so intense that she clawed at his back to keep him from leaving her.

She wanted more.

She wanted Brayden.

He started to move off her, but she grabbed his arms and flipped him to his back. Surprise lit his eyes, and he traced a line down her throat to her breasts. Her nipples hardened to buds, begging for his mouth.

But it was time to give him pleasure.

She kissed him again, then lowered her body on top of him and stroked his thick length against her warm center. She wanted him inside her.

He kissed her deeply, then gently pushed her away.

"Brayden?"

He held up a finger, then reached into his nightstand and snagged a condom. Relieved he wasn't ending their lovemaking, she snatched the foil packet, ripped it open and rolled it over his rigid length. He grew harder, thicker, and a low growl escaped him as she finished.

"You're torturing me," he said in a husky whisper.

She climbed on top of him, angled her head for another kiss, then impaled herself. Inch by inch, he filled her, stirring her arousal again. He traced a finger over her nipples, then ran his hands over her hips and yanked her harder on top of him.

Passion flared, and a frenzy of need overwhelmed her as they increased the tempo. Skin against skin, lips against lips, bodies dancing in rhythm together... Titillating sensations built within her until they erupted in a firestorm of colors.

Brayden groaned her name, then rolled her to her back and plunged inside her, over and over until he called her name as his own release overcame him.

Mindless with pleasure, they rocked back and forth until the sensations ebbed and slowly subsided. Even then, he wrapped his arms around her and held her so close she could feel his heart beating.

When their breathing steadied, he slipped into the bathroom. A minute later, when he returned he dragged her into his arms again. She curled next to him, taking solace in his strength.

Thoughts of DiSanti threatened, and she kissed him once more, then crawled down his body to take his length into her mouth. Brayden groaned and protested, but she brought him to arousal again, then he rolled her to the side and made love to her.

This time when she came, emotions and exhaustion mingled, and she collapsed against him.

As long as she closed her eyes and felt him next to her, she could convince herself that everything would be all right.

Eventually, she fell asleep, a deep sleep where she

dreamed that Izzy was home and that Brayden was in their lives and they were a family.

BRAYDEN LISTENED TO Mila's labored breathing for a long time. She had to be exhausted from the emotional strain of the last couple of days. Making love to her had been mind-blowing.

He cradled her closer, willing her to rest. And for tomorrow to bring them good news about her daughter.

God knows he'd wished this same thing for years where Chrissy was concerned. He prayed for a better outcome with Izzy.

Then what? Mila would return to her life with her daughter. And he would go back to his life. Alone.

Except the thought of that disturbed him.

He liked Mila. He wanted her to have her daughter. But he wanted to be in their lives, as well.

Would she have room for him once Izzy was returned?

And what if he couldn't deliver on his promise to bring Izzy home safely?

He had to...

For hours, he lay in bed contemplating what he should be doing differently on the case. How he could find DiSanti.

Hours later, he drifted to sleep, but a loud knock jerked him awake. He blinked, confused for a moment, then saw Mila asleep in his bed, and memories of the night before returned. Sweet, blissful, erotic memories of lovemaking that he wanted to repeat.

The pounding sounded again.

Mila stirred, but he pulled the covers over her, and

crawled from bed. He yanked on jeans and a T-shirt, then padded into the den. Another knock and he swung open the door.

Lucas.

He looked angry.

"What's going on?" Brayden asked as Lucas stormed past him.

Lucas spun around, arms folded, dark intimidating eyes filled with suspicion. "You tell me."

Brayden scratched his head. His eyes were blurry from lack of sleep.

"Mila has been lying to us," Lucas said through gritted teeth.

Brayden glanced at the closed bedroom door, where Mila was still warming his bed. "What are you talking about?"

"The analyst at the Bureau can't find any record of Izzy's birth or of Mila having a child," Lucas said with a dark scowl.

"What? There has to be a mistake," Brayden said.

"Yeah. The mistake is in believing Mila. She's been playing you, Brayden," Lucas said grimly. "Mila isn't just afraid of DiSanti because he threatened her. I think the bastard is Izzy's father."

Chapter Twenty

Brayden stared at his bedroom door, his stomach knotting as Lucas's statement echoed in his head. "What makes you think he's the father?"

"When I saw Izzy's picture," Lucas said, "the similarities struck me. I can't believe you didn't notice."

Because he'd been blinded by Mila.

"So I had my analyst start digging for information. Mila was actually volunteering in Colombia at the same time DiSanti was there four years ago."

Brayden's mind raced, putting the pieces together. If DiSanti was Izzy's father, then Mila had had a relationship with the man.

Had slept with him.

The idea of that monster's hands touching her made him want to punch a wall.

Had she crawled in bed with *him* last night as a distraction to keep him from discovering the truth?

She'd said Izzy's father was dead—which had obviously been a lie. No wonder she'd been secretive and uncooperative when Lucas had arrested her.

Had DiSanti known all along that Izzy was his daughter and taken her because she belonged to him?

Had Mila lied about being coerced to perform the surgery, too? Had she helped DiSanti escape because they had a child together?

A sense of betrayal cut thought Brayden like a sharp knife. He was a fool. Had done the very thing he knew not to do—he'd fallen for a client and been used again.

Brayden made the mistake of glancing at his closed bedroom door, and Lucas paced in front of the fireplace. "Good God, don't tell me you slept with her. What the hell were you thinking, Brayden?"

That I wanted her and admired her and thought we might have something special.

Idiot.

The door to his bedroom squeaked open, and Mila appeared, her hair tousled. She had dressed in jeans and a flannel shirt, and dammit, she looked beautiful.

But her wary gaze met his. Had she heard their conversation?

"Dr. Manchester," Lucas said, eyebrows arched in question. "Maybe you should join us."

Mila gave a little nod and entered the room, her expression wary. "Did you find Izzy?"

Lucas shook his head no. "But I did learn some interesting information about your daughter's father."

Brayden held his breath, hoping Lucas was wrong. That there was another explanation other than Mila being with DiSanti.

But she heaved a breath and averted her gaze for a brief second, and he had his answer.

"You…and DiSanti," Brayden said, the harsh words erupting. "You lied to me, used me."

Mila shook her head and walked toward him, but he

threw up a hand, warning her to stop. She halted, then lifted her chin. "It's not what you think."

"What I think is that you had a relationship with that bastard, then helped him escape to protect your little girl's father." Disappointment mushroomed inside him. "How did you meet and get involved? Did you know who he was and what he was doing when you were together?"

Mila glared at him and then Lucas, then folded her arms. "You have it all wrong. I wasn't involved with DiSanti."

Brayden simply waited. "But you—"

"I told you it's not what you think," Mila said flatly.

He and Lucas exchanged confused looks. Then a sickening thought occurred to Brayden. "Mila...he didn't...force you, did he?"

Mila's face turned ashen, and she walked to the French doors and looked out at the back deck. Brayden's heart hammered. Lucas stood still, his body tense as they waited.

Brayden crossed the room to Mila, took a deep breath and gently turned her to face him. He braced himself for the gory details. "Tell me the truth. What happened?"

"It wasn't me," Mila said in a low voice.

He narrowed his eyes. "What do you mean, it wasn't you?"

"DiSanti didn't rape *me*," she said, emphasizing the word *me*.

"I don't understand," Brayden said.

"Just tell us the truth this time," Lucas interjected. "We've wasted enough time on your lies."

Mila swayed backward as if she'd been punched.

Brayden was angry, too, but he gave his brother a warning look. Mila might have lied to them, but the terror in her expression was real. "Please, Mila, I told you that you could trust me, and you can."

Indecision warred in her eyes. "It's complicated."

"Is DiSanti Izzy's father?" he asked through gritted teeth.

Mila closed her eyes as if pained, then opened them and gave a wary nod. "Yes, but I'm not her birth mother."

Shock slammed into Brayden. That was the last thing he'd expected to hear.

And it complicated everything. If Mila wasn't Izzy's mother, then who was? Worse, DiSanti had kidnapped his own child, meaning they had no legal recourse to take her from the man.

MILA'S HEART ACHED at the look of betrayal on Brayden's face. She'd never wanted to lie to him, but she had to protect her daughter at all costs.

But now her secret was out.

What would Lucas and Brayden do with it?

Brayden suddenly swung away from her, disappointment and anger radiating from him. "I need caffeine."

Lucas remained pensive as Brayden started a pot of coffee, making her even more antsy. She had no idea what was going on in that head of his.

Brayden poured coffee in mugs, then brought Lucas and her one. She sank onto the sofa and cradled the cup between her hands to warm herself as she struggled to find a way to begin.

Brayden returned for a mug for himself, then joined them, the tension thick.

"Tell us what happened," Lucas said. "You took DiSanti's baby?"

Mila sipped her coffee, then decided to tell him everything. She might be in trouble, but the most important thing was saving Izzy from that horrible man. "You asked if I was raped and I told you no. But Izzy's birth mother was one of DiSanti's victims."

Brayden hissed between his teeth at the image she painted.

"Go on," Lucas said.

The memory of Carina coming to her that rainy night flashed back, stirring pain and fear. "The girl's name was Carina," Mila said. "I met her at the clinic after she escaped DiSanti. She was pregnant and alone and terrified. She had no place to go, so I arranged for her to stay in a shelter."

"She could have come to us," Lucas said. "If she'd testified, we could have protected her."

Mila swallowed back disgust. "You don't understand how terrified and traumatized she was. She was a little girl herself. She'd been drugged and forced to entertain men. Then DiSanti decided he wanted her for himself." She sipped her coffee again, the chill inside her growing more intense at the memory. "He locked her in his private lair and raped her repeatedly."

Silence, thick and filled with the horror of her words, stretched between them for several seconds.

Lucas cleared his throat. "How did she get away from DiSanti?"

Mila traced a finger around the rim of her mug. "She

said the minute she realized she was pregnant, that she decided she had to leave. She didn't want him to know about the baby." She paused, thinking about how frightened Carina must have been. And how brave.

"DiSanti traveled a lot," she continued. "One night when he was gone, she sneaked out the window. She said she ran for miles and miles. His men came after her, but she hid in a drainpipe, then an abandoned mine for days with no food. She drank water from a nearby creek at night when she thought no one was looking for her."

Emotions twisted Brayden's face, but he didn't comment.

"Then what?" Lucas asked.

"One night she hitched a ride to Austin. By then, she was feverish and dehydrated. A woman picked her up and brought her to my clinic. She was terrified and so alone, but eventually she told me her story."

"You knew who DiSanti was?" Lucas asked.

Mila nodded. "I'd heard his name floating around in relation to human trafficking." Mila released a pent-up breath. "When she was feeling better, I helped Carina move into a shelter. In the past three years, two more girls escaped DiSanti and showed up at the clinic. I helped them find a safe place, as well."

Brayden finally spoke. "Good God, Mila, does DiSanti know all this?"

"When he showed up at my clinic for the surgery, he said I'd taken girls away from him and that I owed him."

"That's the reason he chose you for the cosmetic surgery," Brayden said, as if it made sense now.

"Did DiSanti know about Izzy?" Lucas asked.

She shook her head. "I don't think so. At least, he didn't mention her or her mother."

"No doubt he would have if he'd known," Lucas said.

Mila nodded. "He would probably have killed me right after I finished the surgery."

A strained silence fell between them, mired in the truth of her statement.

Brayden shifted. "So how did you come to have Izzy?"

Mila rubbed her temple where a headache was staring to pulse. "One rainy night shortly after Izzy was born, Carina showed up at my door. She said the people at the shelter found a home where she could live and attend school. She knew she was too young to raise a child on her own and wanted to make a future for herself. Then she begged me to take Izzy and raise her." Her voice cracked. "What was I supposed to do?" she said in a raw whisper. "I couldn't turn her away or let that little baby go into the system. And I sure as hell couldn't let DiSanti have her."

Only now he did.

"Do you know where DiSanti is or where he was going?" Brayden asked.

Mila gaped at him. "Of course not. If I did, I would have told you."

"Did Carina sign Izzy over to you? Did you file adoption papers?" Brayden asked.

Mila chewed the inside of her cheek. There was no use lying. He would find out that there was no official adoption. "No, she was scared and in a hurry when she left. I was afraid if I filed for adoption, that DiSanti would discover the truth and come after Izzy."

Brayden cursed, then stood and walked to the French doors. She wanted to join him, to ask him to forgive her for keeping secrets.

But he obviously didn't want to hear it.

Lucas cleared his throat. "Have you been in touch with him since we left the FBI field office?"

Mila glanced down at her hands again. She wanted to trust them, to tell them about the text.

But DiSanti had her little girl. And she couldn't do anything to jeopardize Izzy's life.

So she shook her head no.

BRAYDEN NEEDED TIME to assimilate everything Mila had confessed.

Faced with the fact that she'd lied to him, he didn't know whether to trust her now. She'd bent the truth to help Izzy and her young mother, or at least that's what she wanted them to believe.

The Mila he thought he knew would have done that.

But for some reason, he sensed she was still holding back.

Not to mention she'd broken the law. Technically DiSanti had legal rights to his daughter whereas Mila could be charged with kidnapping.

He believed in upholding the law, but this time there were grays. Mila's daughter was an innocent, trusting little girl.

How could he put her back in the hands of the monster who sold and traded young girls and women?

Lucas's phone buzzed, and he stepped aside to answer it.

"I'm sorry, Brayden," Mila said. "I wanted to tell you everything that day at the FBI office, but I was afraid."

"Afraid you'd go to jail for kidnapping?" Brayden asked, his voice harsher than he'd intended.

Hurt flashed across Mila's face. "No, afraid DiSanti would learn about Izzy. If you'd seen this thirteen-year-old girl, beaten and bruised and terrified of DiSanti, you'd understand."

He had seen Evie, Mae Lynn, Adrian and Agnes. "You should have trusted me to understand."

Mila shrugged. "All I wanted to do was help Carina recover and have a future. That's what she wanted for her baby, too." She touched his arm. "What else could I have done?"

A muscle ticked in Brayden's jaw. Before he could respond, Lucas stepped back inside. "I have to go. Charlotte is on her way to pick you up, Mila. One of the girls at the hospital wants to talk to you."

"Does she have information?" Brayden asked.

"I don't know," Lucas said, "but they opened up to Charlotte and Mila yesterday. Maybe one of them remembered something helpful." He gestured to his phone. "Meanwhile, forensics identified a print from Dr. Manchester's house. Belongs to a man associated with Jameson Beck. I'm going to question him."

Brayden couldn't just sit around. He wanted to do something.

And he needed space from Mila. Although he understood her reasons for keeping secrets, it hurt that she hadn't trusted him.

Especially after the night before.

A knock sounded, and Brayden let Charlotte in. She

took one look across the room and must have felt the tension. "Should I come back?"

Mila shook her head no. "Let me freshen up. I'll be right back." She ducked into the guest room and the shower water kicked on.

"What's going on?" Charlotte asked.

Lucas explained the situation while Brayden cleaned up in his bathroom. Ten minutes later, he was ready. Mila emerged about the same time. She'd pulled her hair back into a low ponytail, and looked young and vulnerable, and so damn sad that he wanted to draw her in his arms again and make love to her until they both forgot the obstacles between them.

But he was done playing the fool.

As soon as they got Izzy back, figured out what to do with her and captured DiSanti, she'd be out of his life.

Chapter Twenty-One

Mila's nerves were on edge as Charlotte drove toward the hospital. Her friend turned into the parking lot of a small diner before they arrived and cut the engine.

"Come on, we're stopping for a hot breakfast," Charlotte said. "You look like you need it."

Mila swallowed the lump in her throat. She needed her daughter back. "I'm really not hungry."

Charlotte touched her arm and offered her a stern look. "You may not be, but you need to eat and keep up your strength."

Tears blurred Mila's eyes. "I can't believe you're being so nice to me. Aren't you angry like Lucas and Brayden?"

Charlotte's heartfelt sigh mirrored the tender understanding in her eyes. "How can I be mad at you for protecting your child?"

Mila bit her lip. "Didn't Lucas tell you the rest?"

Charlotte squeezed Mila's hand between her own. "What? That DiSanti is her father?"

Mila nodded miserably. "Her mother—"

"Was a terrified young girl who was raped," Charlotte said. "For that alone, DiSanti needs to go to prison.

And then there's all his other crimes. When I think of what he did to Evie and Mae Lynn and Adrian and Agnes, I get riled up all over again."

"She was so scared when she came to me," Mila said softly.

"And brave," Charlotte said. "She escaped him, and she did the most unselfish thing anyone can do. She must have loved the baby to give her up."

"She wanted her to have a better life," Mila said. "And I wanted that for both of them."

"I know you did," Charlotte said softly. "And I promise that we'll find Izzy, and she'll have a future with you."

"But Brayden looked so hurt, and they're both furious that I didn't tell them the truth sooner." Mila gulped. "And technically Izzy isn't mine. What if I get her back and they take her away from me?"

Charlotte hissed between her teeth. "Don't worry about that. The Hawk men may be miffed now, but they're the most protective bunch of males I've ever met. They won't let DiSanti keep Izzy. And they'd never let anyone take a baby out of her mama's arms."

She released her hand. "Except legally I'm not her mama."

"You are in every way that counts," Charlotte assured her. "The rest is paperwork. And Brayden is excellent at cutting through red tape." She opened her car door and motioned for Mila to follow. "Now, let's grab some breakfast before we visit the girls. It's going to be another long day."

Mila checked her phone as she got out and said a prayer that she'd hear something today.

She didn't know how much more waiting she could take.

BRAYDEN'S EMOTIONS BOOMERANGED all over the place. Dammit, he still wanted to help Mila. And he sure as hell wanted to save Izzy from DiSanti.

"I know you're upset, brother," Lucas said. "I didn't realize you and the doctor had gotten…chummy."

Brayden silently cursed. "It just happened. She was upset, worried. I wanted to comfort her."

Lucas pulled down a side street. "You sleep with all your clients to comfort them?"

Anger flared inside Brayden. "That's not fair, man. You slept with Charlotte."

Lucas grimaced. "For the record, I'm not proud of the fact that I was on the job." A smile tugged at his mouth. "That said, I'm not sorry it happened though. She's the best thing that ever happened to me."

That was true.

For a second last night, Brayden had entertained the idea that Mila was his Charlotte.

Fool.

Brayden scanned the parking lot of the feed store where this guy Theo was supposed to be working. "Once we catch DiSanti and rescue Izzy, what's going to happen to Izzy?"

Lucas shifted the vehicle into Park and cut the engine. "Let's just get him and save Izzy. Then we'll discuss where to go from there."

What more could Brayden ask for?

For Lucas not to arrest Mila for kidnapping? Technically she hadn't… In her situation, he would have done the same thing. And no way would Lucas have let that baby be carted off by DiSanti.

Lucas climbed out, and Brayden followed him up to the door of the feed store. The store looked empty, a truck parked to the side by a loading dock. Brayden took a few steps and noticed more trucks in the back at the loading dock. Voices echoed from the dock, and cigarette smoke curled into the air near the rear door.

He motioned to Lucas that he was heading that way while his brother strode inside the store. He dug his hands into the pockets of his jacket and adjusted his Stetson, glad he'd worn jeans and a T-shirt and cowboy boots. Sometimes the suit was intimidating.

Two men looked up and went still, their conversation quieting.

A big burly guy in a jean jacket and battered boots sauntered toward him, his posture defensive. Brayden wasn't a small guy, but this man probably outweighed him by fifty pounds and carried himself like a street fighter. "What can we do for you, mister?"

Brayden tilted his hat to the side. "Looking for Theo Reeves? Is that you?"

The guy's brows pinched together. "Who's asking?"

It was Reeves. Damn. Brayden had to stall. He might need backup. He moved forward, lifting his chin. "I'm looking for a missing kid. A three-year-old little girl named Izzy Manchester. I think you know where she is."

Panic flashed across the brawny man's face. "Don't know what the hell you're talking about."

"Really?" Lucas appeared from the back door. "Because your print showed up at her house. The very house where she was abducted at gunpoint."

The man's gaze shot from Lucas to him, then he growled and broke into a run. Lucas raised his gun and shouted for the man to stop, but Reeves dived into the driver's side of a feed truck.

Brayden was closer and jogged after him, then yanked at the door as the man started the engine. The engine fired up, and Theo started to back away.

Lucas fired a shot at the tires. Brayden yanked at the car door and pulled it open. Theo punched him in the face, and Brayden's head jerked backward. Dammit, he didn't intend to let this bastard get the best of him.

Mila and Izzy needed him.

He clutched the door and grabbed Theo's beefy arm. But Theo lifted his free hand and raised a gun with it, pointing it straight at Brayden.

Brayden cursed and reached for his own, but the man pushed the gun at Brayden's temple, and he froze.

A second later, a bullet whizzed by his head. Theo's body bounced backward, and blood spurted from his forehead where Lucas's bullet had hit its mark.

MILA HADN'T THOUGHT she could eat, but she felt marginally better after a hearty breakfast and coffee. Still, the uncertainty of where Izzy was and what Brayden and Lucas planned needled her.

When they arrived at the hospital, she checked on Keenan and Anita and Frannie while Charlotte went to visit the two other victims.

Keenan was sitting up and looked more rested and

focused, as if the last of the drugs had been flushed from her system.

"Did you find Izzy?" Keenan asked.

Mila shook her head. "Not yet."

Keenan twisted the sheets between her fingers. "I remembered something else. I don't know if it's important or not."

Mila stroked the girl's shoulder. "Even the smallest detail might help, sweetie."

"I heard them talking about a plane."

"You mean a flight they were going to catch?"

Keenan shook her head. "I think it was a small plane. A private one."

Mila sucked in a sharp breath. Of course, DiSanti had the money for a private jet. It also made it easier for him to escape.

"Did they mention where they were flying?"

Keenan shook her head. "They said they had to wait until he was feeling better."

"He?"

"They didn't use his name. But I knew who they were talking about."

Mila's phone vibrated in her pocket. She grabbed it and checked the screen.

You aren't listening, Dr. Manchester. I thought you wanted to see your daughter again.

Fear caught in her throat. She told Keenan she'd be right back. She walked down the hall to the vending machine then sent a return text to DiSanti, but the text immediately bounced back.

She made a pained sound, barely stifling a scream. A footstep sounded behind her. She started to spin around to see who was there, but something sharp jabbed her in the back.

Then a man's low growl in her ear, "If you scream or try to alert someone, the kid is dead."

Mila went perfectly still. "I'll do whatever you say, just don't hurt my daughter."

"Then walk."

Mila forced a breath in and out, then did as he ordered. She passed two nurses she recognized from the night before, then ducked into the elevator. The man holding the gun on her remained close behind her, the barrel of his gun digging into her back.

Her heart pounded when a janitor and a young couple with a baby entered the elevator. The baby in the pink blanket reminded her of her daughter.

The janitor narrowed his eyes at her as if he recognized her, maybe from the night before, but she simply smiled at him, then pretended interest in her phone.

The doors whooshed open on the second floor, and the janitor exited. The couple followed, and she was left alone with the man and his gun. He ordered her toward an exit, and she walked on unsteady legs to the door.

Outside, the skies had turned a dark gray, and the wind had picked up as if a storm was brewing. Mila stumbled as he pushed her forward, then caught herself and walked on.

A white van pulled up in front of the emergency room door, and the man shoved her toward it. A second later, the side door opened and he pushed her inside.

As soon as she fell onto the floor, someone dragged a bag over her head.

Then she felt a hard whack to the back of her skull, and the world went black.

LUCAS STAYED WITH Reeves's body until the ME arrived while Brayden checked in with Dexter. Nothing new. Dammit.

Lucas's cell phone buzzed. "Charlotte," he said, then connected the call.

Maybe one of the girls at the hospital had offered some new information.

Lucas scowled, then cursed. "All right. I'll see if we can trace her phone."

A bad feeling shot through Brayden.

"Call me if you hear anything." Lucas hung up, his expression grave.

"What's going on?" Brayden asked.

"Mila's gone."

Brayden's lungs tightened. "What do you mean *gone*?"

"She and Charlotte had breakfast on the way to the hospital, then split up to talk to the girls," Lucas said. "When Charlotte went to find Mila, she saw her at the end of the hall leaving with a man."

Fear robbed Brayden's response.

"Charlotte called security, but by the time they showed up, Mila was outside. The guard saw a man push Mila into the back of a van."

Brayden released a string of expletives. "Did security get the license plate?"

Lucas shook his head. "Apparently there wasn't one."

Brayden pinched the bridge of his nose. This couldn't be happening. He'd promised Mila he'd protect her and bring Izzy back to her, but now DiSanti's men had them both.

"What now?" Brayden said. "We've exhausted our leads."

Lucas gave him a big brother look. "Don't give up. I'll call our analyst and see if she can trace Mila's phone. Charlotte said Keenan mentioned hearing the men talk about a private airplane. I'll get our people looking into that."

"Don't you think it's time to go wide with the media on this?" Brayden said. "We kept quiet because of Mila. But we need any lead we can get."

"That would help," Lucas said. "Or it could spook DiSanti into killing Mila."

Emotions crowded Brayden's chest. "We both know he's probably going to kill Mila anyway. If DiSanti knows Izzy is his child, he's probably furious and out for blood."

Lucas nodded. "You're right. I'll issue an Amber Alert for Izzy and send her picture and Mila's out to the media and all the authorities."

Desperation made sweat break out on Brayden's neck. They had to find Mila and Izzy before it was too late.

MILA'S HEAD THROBBED as she roused from unconsciousness. She rolled to her side and realized she was still in the back of the van, the hood over her head.

The van bounced over potholes and tossed her against the side of the vehicle. The floor was cold, hard.

She forced herself to listen for sounds that might indicate where they were taking her. A bus? Train? Traffic? Planes?

Nothing but dead quiet and the chug of the engine.

Fear mingled with relief that she would at least get to see Izzy again. But what would happen then?

Her phone vibrated in her pocket, but her hands were bound, and she couldn't get to it. Had Charlotte realized she was gone by now? Was Brayden looking for her?

The van rolled to a stop, brakes squealing, then the door screeched open. Cold hard hands grabbed her and she fought, but he dug in her pocket, grabbed her phone, then slammed the door again.

Tears pricked her eyes. Brayden and Lucas could have traced her with the phone, but the brute had probably tossed it.

The engine started up again and roared away, throwing her across the back of the van. They rode for what seemed like forever before tires ground on the graveled road, and the van bounced to a stop.

She waited on it to start up again, but it didn't. Instead, the van door screeched open, and the brute yanked her from the back of the vehicle. She stumbled, willing him to remove the hood, but he dragged her forward, keeping her in the dark.

Thunder rumbled, then another male voice echoed in the distance.

She struggled to remain upright, her feet slipping and clawing at the rough gravel as they climbed a hill. A minute later, she heard another door open, then the man pushed her forward. The ground turned to a wooden floor, and they were walking. A hall?

Another male voice echoed in the distance, but her

abductor yanked her arm again. Her feet grappled for control as she struggled to keep up with him.

A door creaked open, then he pushed her again, this time so hard that she stumbled. With her hands tied and face covered, she lost her balance and completely collapsed onto the floor.

The door slammed shut.

She cried out in frustration, but a low whisper rose from the corner. She went still.

Then shuffling and someone was lifting the hood from her head. She blinked into the darkness, disoriented, heaving a breath.

The person who'd removed her hood slowly slipped into focus.

"Dr. Manchester," the girl whispered.

Shock hit her like a fist in the gut. "Carina?"

Tears trickled from the young girl's terrified eyes. She was bruised and battered, but she was here.

"How? Why?"

"He found me," she said on a ragged whisper. "He knows everything."

Chapter Twenty-Two

Mila tried not to react, but then she saw Izzy curled in the corner, trembling, curled in a fetal position, and her composure crumbled.

"Untie me," Mila cried. "I have to get to Izzy."

Carina moved behind Mila and worked the knots in the rope.

"Are you hurt?" Mila asked. "Did they hurt Izzy?"

"We're both okay," Carina said softly. "They didn't hurt her. She's just scared and misses you."

The tenderness in the girl's eyes made Mila's heart ache. Carina had probably earned those bruises protecting Izzy.

"She's beautiful," Carina said as she finished untying Mila.

Mila shook the feeling back into her fingers and hugged Carina. "Yes, she is. Now we have to get her away from DiSanti and his men."

How she was going to do that she didn't know.

She crawled toward her daughter, her heart racing. "Izzy, it's Mommy," she whispered. "I'm here."

She gently stroked Izzy's soft hair away from her face, and Izzy lifted her head. When she saw Mila, her eyes widened, and she threw her arms around Mila, her little body shaking.

Mila cradled her daughter against her, then rocked her while she cried. Her own tears blended with Izzy's, then Carina was beside them, and she pulled the young mother up against them.

"WE HAVE AN ADDRESS," Lucas said as he and Brayden sped down the road. "Mila must have left her phone on so we could trace it."

Thank God she was smart. He just hoped she was still alive.

He said prayer after prayer as Lucas careened around a corner and sped onto a graveled road.

Brayden's phone buzzed. He checked it, hoping for a miracle. Not Mila though. A number he didn't recognize.

He pressed Connect. "Brayden Hawk."

Silence. Breathing.

"Hello? Who is this?"

"Mr. Hawk?"

Brayden stilled. The voice sounded familiar. "Yes."

"It's Jorge."

The ranch hand that worked for Corley. "I'm really busy, Jorge, so unless you called to help—"

"I did," Jorge said in a muffled voice as if he didn't want anyone to hear him. "Did you mean what you said about helping my family?"

Lucas glanced over at him with a raised brow, then slowed as they neared an abandoned stretch of land. Boulders created a natural landmark where the road forked.

"Yes, I meant it. I'll do whatever I can to make sure your family is safe and you're with them," Brayden said.

"I saw the news. Is it true that this man DiSanti kidnapped Dr. Manchester?"

"It's true. She and her daughter are both in danger. Now, tell me what you know."

Jorge cleared his throat. "I heard Mr. Corley talking on the phone. He said they needed to move the merchandise, to get the contacts in Juarez ready."

So Corley was involved. "Did he say where the merchandise is being held?"

"No. But Mr. Corley told him to take care of his problem before he flew out."

Keenan had mentioned a private plane. "Anything else?"

"He said he didn't want the feds breathing down his neck." Jorge paused again, static on the line as if he was muffling his voice. "He's back. I have to go."

"Thanks, Jorge. I'll be in touch about your family."

The phone clicked silent.

Lucas screeched to a stop at the group of boulders, then climbed out.

"What are we doing?" Brayden asked as he joined his brother.

Lucas's dark scowl tracked the area as if searching for something. "This is where the trace ended."

Brayden's heart clamored. Either Mila's phone had been tossed here… Or her body had.

MILA WIPED AWAY Izzy's tears. "I'm here now, honey. I've been looking for you, and I'm going to find a way to take us home."

Carina was watching Izzy with a mixture of love and sadness in her eyes.

"All of us," Mila said, knowing she couldn't abandon the girl who'd given birth to Izzy.

The door suddenly opened, and a big barrel of a man with black hair and black eyes strode into the room. He was heavily armed.

Without a word, he jerked Mila to a standing position. "DiSanti needs you, Dr. Manchester."

Mila fought a cry of terror. Was he going to kill her now? If so, what would happen to Izzy?

She and Carina traded an understanding look—they would both protect Izzy with their lives.

She held up a finger to the man. "Just one second." She jerked away, then stooped and gave Izzy another hug and a kiss. "I love you, sweetie. You and Carina hang tight while I take care of my patient." She squeezed Carina's hand, déjà vu taking her back to the night Carina brought Izzy to her door.

If she died, Lucas and Brayden would keep looking for Izzy. Maybe they could help Carina, too.

The man grunted, then motioned it was time for her to go. She grappled for courage, then stood and followed him out the door on wobbly legs.

Without the bag over her head, she took inventory of her surroundings as they walked down the hall. The house was an older ranch, wood floors, rooms on both sides of a kitchen in the center. Through the windows, she spotted acres and acres of farmland.

They were in the middle of nowhere.

How would Lucas and Brayden ever find them?

A noise sounded, and she hesitated, then realized it was the sound of a small airplane. DiSanti's private jet.

The brute with the gun gestured for her to walk down the hall, and she entered a large room with a king-size bed. The double window offered a view of a landing strip.

Against the wall stood a steel table with medical supplies and bandages. A woman dressed in a nurse's uniform was jotting notes on a clipboard. She must have been caring for DiSanti. But the bed was empty.

Then Mila saw DiSanti. He was sitting in a chair in the corner, hidden in the shadows. His face still looked puffy and slightly red, but she had to admit that he was some of her best work. If she didn't know who he was, she wouldn't have recognized him.

DiSanti looked up at her with cold, rage-filled eyes, then stood and walked toward her, his shoulders rigid. "You stole my daughter," he said. "Now you know what that feels like."

Mila inhaled a fortifying breath. "Her mother wanted her to have a future, to be raised in a normal, safe environment."

The man raised his hand and slapped her across the face. She stumbled backward.

"She's mine and she belongs with me," he growled.

"Why?" Mila asked sharply. "So you can sell her or turn her into a sex slave for a monster like yourself?"

Another blow, this one so sharp and hard that her face stung, and she tasted blood. Then another one and another until Mila fell to her knees, the world spinning.

BRAYDEN RELAYED HIS conversation with Jorge to Lucas, and Lucas phoned his analyst at the FBI to search for a location that might house a private runway. While he spoke with her, Brayden began to search the area for Mila's phone, praying she was still alive.

The land was parched, although gray skies above threatened a downpour. He had to hurry before the clouds unloaded.

Tumbleweed blew across the terrain, miles and miles of desolate land stretching before them. He checked around the boulders, but didn't find a phone or any signs of Mila. No footprints either, meaning the men hadn't gotten out of the vehicle.

Of course, they could have simply slowed and pushed her body out of the van, but why would they do it in an open area? Granted, this property was off the grid, but DiSanti's men would most likely have found a ravine or wooded area, someplace not easily detectable.

God… He had to stop thinking like that. Mila was not dead. She couldn't be.

He loved her too much to lose her.

Love?

He kicked gravel from his boot. He had no time to think about love when Mila's and Izzy's lives hung in the balance.

He walked along the edge of the road, searching the bushes and weeds and the ditch, then crossed the road to the opposite side. About six feet down, something shiny glinted against the dirt.

He jogged toward it, then knelt and dug the phone from the foliage. A quick examination confirmed it was Mila's.

He brushed it off and yelled to Lucas that he'd found the phone as he headed back toward his brother.

Lucas nodded. "I don't think Mila's here. They probably just dumped her phone to throw us off." His phone buzzed and Lucas skimmed a text, then motioned for Brayden to get in the car. "Let's go. I have the location of an abandoned ranch equipped with its own runway. It's not far from here."

Brayden's pulse hammered as he buckled up, and Lucas sped away. Gravel spewed behind them as Lucas careened down the road. The scenery whisked by in a blur.

Minutes dragged into half an hour, making Brayden's nerves more frazzled. He thought they'd never get there, but finally the property appeared in the distance. The ranch was enormous, with acres and acres of unused land. Wild mustangs galloped on a hill in the distance, the land beginning to roll into hills as it stretched for miles.

Lucas slowed as he turned down the drive, he and Brayden alert in case DiSanti's men were watching.

A mile onto the property, and someone shot at the car. Lucas swerved to the right, and Brayden rolled down his window and fired. One shot, two. He hit the bastard who was perched on the back of a flatbed truck.

Anger coiled inside him, and Lucas was stone-faced, his hands clenching the steering wheel in a white-knuckled grip. Another mile and Brayden spotted the farmhouse, a giant rambling structure that had seen better days.

Set back here in the middle of nowhere, it was the perfect place to hide. Another reason DiSanti had chosen Texas. Its vastness alone offered a multitude of remote locations, undeveloped properties and abandoned farms.

Lucas parked a half mile from the house, and the two of them got out, both armed and alert.

A gunshot blasted the air, and Brayden ducked. Lucas spun to the left and fired, nailing the shooter, who'd been hiding in a thicket of trees.

They crept closer, weaving between the bushes bordering the drive, then slipped up to the house.

More gunshots. Two men firing from the barn by the house. Lucas fired back and had to roll in the dirt to dodge a bullet.

An engine sounded from the back of the house. The plane.

Dammit.

Lucas shook his head, warning Brayden to stay put, but Brayden ignored him and raced around the side of the house. Lucas was right on his tail, and they made it to the back just as three big gunmen emerged, guarding DiSanti.

Brayden wanted to shoot him then, but they had to find Mila.

The back door opened, and two men hurried out, dragging someone with them.

Dear God. Mila. She was beaten and limp, her hair tangled around her bloody face.

Behind them another man hauled a too-thin teenage girl beside him. She looked frail and frightened but clutched a little girl—Izzy, it had to be—in her arms. Izzy had her head buried against the teen, obviously terrified.

If DiSanti had hurt Izzy, Brayden would kill him with his bare hands.

Lucas motioned for Brayden to follow his lead, then Lucas identified himself and ordered the men to halt or he'd shoot.

They didn't listen. They opened fire, and all hell broke loose. Lucas took cover behind a bush and fired at the men while Brayden aimed his gun at the man holding the teenage girl and Izzy.

He didn't take time to analyze what he was doing. He was going to save that kid.

He fired at the bastard and nailed him in the head. The big man's body bounced back with a grunt, then he dropped to the ground like a rock.

Brayden motioned for the girl and Izzy to run. Just as they did, Lucas fired at the men holding Mila, but the men dodged the bullet and dragged Mila toward the plane.

Two more shooters fired from behind barrels stacked next to the hangar, forcing Brayden and Lucas to duck to avoid being hit.

Another shot from the right, and Brayden swung around and fired, hitting the shooter and taking him out.

Lucas caught the big guy in the shoulder, and Mila suddenly shoved the other man to the ground and ran toward her daughter and the teen.

The bastard rolled on the ground and lifted his weapon again. Brayden fired, but the man managed to get off a round first.

At the same time, Izzy started running toward Mila. Panic seared Brayden. No… Izzy was in the line of fire.

The teen suddenly threw herself in front of Izzy.

The bullet hit her in the back, and she collapsed to the ground, shielding Izzy with her body. Brayden nailed him, but the damage was done.

Mila screamed and dived for Izzy and the girl while Lucas raced toward the plane.

The door to the plane closed, the engine roared and the plane sped down the runway.

Lucas chased the plane, shooting at it, but the plane soared into the sky. Brayden ran to Mila. She was sobbing and lifting the limp teenager away from Izzy.

Brayden knelt and helped her roll the girl off Izzy, and Mila pulled Izzy into her arms, frantically checking her for injuries.

Izzy was wide-eyed in shock, still clinging to the young teen. Mila dragged the girl into her lap so she could hold both her and Izzy.

Then the girl's eyes fluttered open and she looked up at Mila.

"Take care of our little girl," Carina whispered.

Mila sobbed the girl's name and promised that she would.

Chapter Twenty-Three

Brayden held Mila and Izzy while they waited for an ambulance. Mila was devastated over Carina's death. What a senseless loss.

Even after all she'd suffered, Carina had loved that child.

And he had overheard Carina ask Mila to take care of her daughter. He'd use that in court as leverage to file adoption papers. Although getting DiSanti to release his rights would be difficult—maybe impossible.

He would figure out the details later. For now, he was grateful Mila and Izzy had survived.

Although seeing Mila battered and beaten tore him in knots. Lucas called reinforcements to take care of the bodies and his people were working on tracking DiSanti's plane.

But he might be long gone.

Mila and Izzy wouldn't be safe until he was locked away—or dead.

Brayden would prefer the latter. In fact, he'd like to be the one to put a bullet in DiSanti's head.

When the ambulance arrived, Brayden stepped aside

while they examined Izzy and Mila. True to her nature, Mila was more worried about her daughter than herself.

Lucas approached him, expression stony. "I'll stay here and tie things up at this place if you want to go with Mila and the little girl to the hospital."

Brayden murmured agreement. His emotions were wreaking havoc with his nerves.

"Who was the teenager?" Lucas asked. "One of Di-Santi's victims?"

He nodded. "Izzy's birth mother." That touching exchange had cemented his drive to make sure Mila kept Izzy. "Just before she died, she asked Mila to take care of their little girl."

Lucas raised a brow. "So Mila was telling the truth about the girl giving her Izzy?"

Brayden nodded. "It won't be easy, but I have to figure out a way to make sure Mila is granted legal custody."

A tense silence stretched between them as the medics helped Mila and Izzy into the ambulance and the crime workers arrived to process the scene.

"You know he'll come back for them, Brayden? They won't be safe until we find him."

"I know." Brayden raked a hand through his hair. "We have to protect them, Lucas."

"We will," Lucas assured him.

But Brayden's heart was heavy as he went to join Mila and Izzy.

MILA WAS AN emotional basket case. Carina had died protecting her baby girl.

It wasn't fair.

At the hospital, she assured the staff that she was okay. Bruises would heal. She was far more concerned about the emotional and psychological trauma to Izzy.

At least physically, Izzy was unharmed. Mila cradled her close in the back seat as Brayden drove them to Hawk's Landing. Fearing the house where she'd been abducted might trigger traumatic memories for her daughter, Mila agreed to stay at Brayden's with Izzy, at least for the night.

DiSanti had escaped. Again.

She squeezed Izzy tighter. She couldn't think about that right now. Izzy needed to be comforted and to feel safe.

Carina's face flashed in her mind, and a wave of grief washed over her. One day, she'd tell Izzy the truth about her birth mother, about the selfless, brave love Carina had for her.

Not tonight though.

Brayden steered the SUV down the drive to the ranch, and Izzy clutched Mila's arm. "Where are we going, Mama?"

Mila soothed her with a kiss and stroked her hair. "Brayden is a nice man, honey. He helped me find you. And he's going to let us stay at his ranch for a few days so we can rest."

Fear flickered in Izzy's eyes. "Are the bad men coming back?"

Mila hugged Izzy tighter. "Not tonight, sweetie. We'll be safe at Brayden's ranch."

Izzy stared at her wide-eyed for a moment, then bobbed her head up and down.

"Do they gots horses at the ranch?" Izzy asked.

Mila smiled, grateful that children were resilient. "Yes, they do. Tomorrow we'll ask Brayden if we can see them." She stroked Izzy's hair again. "But tonight we're going to soak in a warm bubble bath and get a good night's sleep." Izzy probably hadn't really slept since she'd been abducted. At least, the doctor confirmed that she hadn't been drugged or molested.

Izzy spied a horse galloping in the pasture nearest the road and squealed in delight.

Mila took it as a good sign that her daughter would be all right, but she would watch for nightmares and signs of anxiety. Brayden had been quiet the entire ride, leaving her wondering what he was thinking.

He'd risked his life to save her and Izzy. His face was bruised, although she had no idea how he'd earned it. She looked worse, but she didn't care.

Tonight Izzy would sleep beside her safe and sound. That was all that mattered.

BRAYDEN COULD BARELY control his rage over the bruises on Mila's face and arms. He wanted to make DiSanti suffer for hurting her.

But she and Izzy had seen enough violence. He inhaled a deep breath as he parked to rein in his temper.

Still, he'd make it his mission to find the bastard and keep him from abusing another girl, woman or child.

He opened the back door for Mila and helped her out of the car, his jaw clenching at the dried blood on her lower lip.

"Do you want me to carry Izzy?" he asked gruffly.

She shook her head no. "Thanks, but I think she needs some alone time with me right now."

That was probably true. But he felt like Mila was shutting him out.

He closed the door after her and hurried to steady her as she climbed the steps with Izzy in her arms.

Izzy looked up at him with wary, big dark eyes as he unlocked the door.

"I heard you like horses," he said with a smile.

Her eyes crinkled with childlike excitement as she bobbed her head up and down.

"Tomorrow I'll take you and your mom around the ranch. You can even pick out one to ride."

"Really?" she asked in such a sweet, innocent voice that she instantly snagged a piece of his heart.

"Really." Mila gave him a grateful smile as they entered.

"Let me know what you need," he said as she carried Izzy toward the bedroom.

"We're going to soak in a nice bath." She looked at her daughter. "Do you want something to eat, sweetie?"

Izzy gave a little nod.

"I don't have much," Brayden said, "except for some frozen mac and cheese."

"I love mac and cheese," Izzy squealed.

"Then mac and cheese it is," he said with a wink.

Mila laughed, and Brayden thought what a beautiful sound. A sound he wanted to hear more often.

Every day.

Deciding Izzy had probably seen enough blood and bruises in her lifetime, he washed up in his bathroom, then took the box of mac and cheese from the freezer and followed the directions to heat it. He also had a frozen pizza so he stuck it in the oven.

Not a gourmet meal, but he had a feeling food wasn't as important tonight as mother and daughter simply being together.

That was what family was about.

Damn. He wanted that family for himself.

Shaken, he stepped onto the back deck for some air.

It was a good half hour before Mila and Izzy emerged from the guest room. Izzy was cocooned in a pair of pink flannel pj's with kitty cats on them, and Mila had dragged on a pair of sweatpants and a long-sleeved T-shirt. Her hair lay in damp strands over her shoulders. She'd dabbed on a little powder to help camouflage the bruises on her face, most likely an effort to spare Izzy.

He lit a fire in the fireplace and made coffee, then set out his brown whiskey and the wine he'd offered Mila before.

They gathered at the farmhouse table by the fire to eat. Izzy looked brighter and surprised him by wolfing down the mac and cheese and a slice of pizza.

Mila laughed as the little girl inhaled a glass of milk on top of it. He had some chocolate chip cookies his mother and the girls at the house had made, and she snatched two of them with a giggle.

Mila sipped a glass of wine after eating, the love in her eyes for her daughter so intense it humbled Brayden and made him forget his anger over the information she'd withheld from him.

But hurt still needled him that she hadn't trusted him.

Izzy yawned, and Mila started to clean up, but he caught her hand and took the plate from her. "I'll handle this. Just enjoy your time with Izzy tonight."

She gave him another grateful look, then scooped Izzy into her arms and carried her to the bedroom. When the door closed behind them, Brayden had a feeling he wouldn't see either one of them until morning.

He cleaned the table and plates, then checked outside to make certain it was quiet. Satisfied DiSanti and his men hadn't had time to track Mila and Izzy to Hawk's Landing, he poured himself a shot of whiskey and carried it to the recliner by the fire.

He stared into the burning embers, his mind contemplating the last few days and all that had happened.

Last night he and Mila had shared the hottest, most mind-boggling sex he'd ever experienced. But it was more than just sex.

He was in love with her.

He had no idea what he was going to do about it though.

Chapter Twenty-Four

Mila savored the next three days at Hawk's Landing. She made arrangements for Roberta and Carina to have proper memorial services and for another doctor to assume her responsibilities at the clinic for a while. She wanted to focus all her energy on being with Izzy.

Her little girl blossomed at the ranch. True to his word, Brayden gave them a ranch tour and helped Izzy choose the tamest riding horse they had for lessons.

Izzy had asked about Roberta and Carina, and about some girl named Jade, who stayed with her when she was abducted.

Brayden and Lucas added Jade to their list of missing girls. Mrs. Hawk also found room for the girls at the hospital to move onto the ranch temporarily. One of her friends had agreed to open her home to them but needed renovations done to make room. Honey volunteered to oversee the project.

The Hawks were amazing people. She understood now why Charlotte had fallen fast and hard for Lucas. And why she loved his family so much.

She watched as Brayden rode Izzy around the riding pen. He was patient and kind and funny. Izzy adored him.

And she was in love with him.

Lucas approached her, his look solemn. Her stomach knotted. She'd hoped every day that he'd find DiSanti so she and Izzy could live free of fear.

He anticipated her question and shook his head no.

She tamped down her sigh of frustration. He was doing everything possible to find the bastard.

But with every passing day, the chances of DiSanti's men finding her at Hawk's Landing increased.

"I appreciate all you and your family have done for me and Izzy," Mila said. "But Izzy and I can't stay here forever."

"You don't like the ranch?" Lucas asked.

Mila sighed. "I love it here, and so does Izzy, but we're imposing on your family." And Brayden. The longer she stayed, the more she didn't want to leave. It was starting to feel like a home, the one she'd always wanted.

"I know you're anxious," Lucas said. "But it's not safe for you to go home yet or back to work."

"As much as I don't like it, I agree." Mila leaned on the rail, soaking in the sight of Izzy with Brayden. The little girl's father was a terrible man and didn't deserve to have a child.

On the other hand, Brayden would make a wonderful father.

She glanced back at the farmhouse and saw Honey in the porch swing chatting with Ava. Evie, Mae Lynn, Adrian and Agnes were showing the new girls their favorite places on the ranch.

Hawk's Landing had become a safe haven for the lost. But she couldn't stay here forever.

"I have to leave," Mila said. "It's too dangerous for your family for me to stay here."

Indecision and regret played across Lucas's face. Charlotte was walking toward them with Mae Lynn, her cheeks rosy with the cold.

The day before Charlotte confided to Mila that she was pregnant. After all she'd been through, she deserved to have her baby and a life with Lucas in peace.

"We don't want you to go," Lucas said.

Mila's heart squeezed. "I appreciate that, Lucas. Your family is the most generous, loving one I've ever known. But that's the reason I *have* to go. DiSanti will use anyone I care about to get to me and Izzy. I won't do that, not to you and Charlotte, or Brayden, or Honey and Harrison or your mother and the girls who escaped him."

Lucas's gaze met hers for a tension-filled moment. Izzy squealed as Brayden swung her down from the palomino he'd chosen for her. Izzy loved that horse and had already started calling the animal hers.

She couldn't allow her daughter to become more attached to this place and these people, then yank her away from this family.

"Will you arrange for us to go into WITSEC?" Mila asked.

Lucas nodded. "I can do that. But you know if you join WITSEC, none of us, including Brayden, can know where you and Izzy are. You'll have to sever all contact with him, and you and Izzy will change your names and go wherever the US Marshals place you. And Mila—"

he hesitated "—you won't be able to practice medicine or do any related kind of work. DiSanti and his men could use that to find you."

Pain washed through Mila, but she murmured that she understood. She'd do whatever necessary to protect Izzy and this family that she'd grown to love.

Even if it meant she couldn't be with them.

Three days later

"Mila, don't go," Brayden said as Mila stood by the car that Lucas had arranged to take her and Izzy away. "I'll do whatever I can to protect you and Izzy."

Mila pressed a hand to Brayden's cheek. "I know you will. That's one reason we have to leave. I won't endanger you and your family."

Emotions darkened Brayden's eyes. "But I love you," he said, his heart pounding with fear. He was losing her, had been arguing with her about this ever since she'd told him her plan.

He had a bone to pick with Lucas, too. His brother had made arrangements with WITSEC without including him in the decision-making process.

"I could go with you," Brayden said. "Then you and Izzy won't be alone."

Mila shook her head. "No. I have to do this by myself, Brayden. Izzy is my family, not yours."

Dammit. Her dig hit home.

He'd professed his love, but she hadn't reciprocated. Because she didn't love him.

That hurt the most.

After all she'd been through, he couldn't force himself on her and her daughter. They needed to be free, even if it meant they needed freedom from him.

He was the fool for falling in love with her.

Emotions clogged his throat. "Will you let me know if you're all right?"

"You know I can't do that," Mila said. "When we leave, it's a clean slate for all of us."

As much as he didn't like it, she was right. Talking to him would only put her in danger. By now, DiSanti and his men might have discovered that he and his family had helped her and given Izzy a home.

He had to let her go to keep her safe.

He opened the car door, where Izzy sat in her car seat, clutching her stuffed animals and pink blanket to her chest. Tears pooled in her big dark eyes.

"I'm going to miss you, sweet pea," he said, then gave her a hug.

She wrapped her arms around him and held him tight, a sob escaping her little body. The precious little girl had definitely stolen his heart.

"I love you," she choked out. "I don't want to leave Blondie." The palomino.

"I love you, too," he murmured, then he pressed a kiss to her hair. "And Blondie will be waiting when you and your mommy can come back."

Mila gave him a warning look as he pulled away.

He didn't know how Mila had survived when Izzy had been in that monster's hands. His heart felt like it was literally breaking into pieces.

Mila gave him a quick kiss on the cheek, then ducked into the car, and the driver sped off.

He watched to see if she looked back at him. But Mila didn't look at him once.

THREE WEEKS LATER, Mila was still crying into her pillow at night.

She didn't dare show her feelings to Izzy, who talked about Brayden and Blondie and the ranch and the Hawk family every single day.

The apartment the US Marshals had put them in was in the middle of this small town in Colorado, far away from Hawk's Landing and the people she loved.

Brayden's face haunted her. She wanted to see him, talk to him, be with him. Every day she relived the sound of his voice telling her that he loved her.

She hadn't said it back. If she'd admitted her feelings out loud, she wouldn't have been able to leave him.

And how could she have asked him to abandon the job and ranch and family that he loved for her? Not when being with her might get him or his mother or family members killed. Ava had lost one child. Mila refused to take away another.

Izzy finished drawing another sketch of Hawk's Landing and the horse she'd ridden. "I miss Blondie, Mommy."

Mila nodded, vying for patience. It wasn't Izzy's fault they were in this mess.

"Do you think Santa will find us here?" Izzy asked in a tiny voice.

Mila pulled Izzy into her lap. "Of course he will, sweetie."

"Will he bring me a puppy?"

Mila hesitated. She hated for Izzy to get attached

to anything else, and then possibly lose it, but she'd be damned if her child would have to sacrifice owning a pet. They couldn't have a horse here, but maybe a puppy...

"Santa knows you're the best girl in the world and he'll remember you on Christmas Eve."

Izzy laid her head back against Mila. "I asked him for something else, too."

Mila closed her eyes and rocked Izzy in her arms. "What was that, sweetie?"

Izzy shrugged. "If I tell you, it won't come true."

Mila kissed her forehead and ran her fingers through her daughter's hair in a loving, soothing gesture. In time, they'd both adjust and accept their new life.

She just wished Brayden was in it.

THANKSGIVING CAME AND WENT. Now it was five days until Christmas. Brayden was miserable.

His family had gathered for their weekly dinner. Lights and decorations adorned the tree. The scent of cinnamon apples and pine filled the air.

Harrison and Honey were cuddled on the couch laughing as they discussed baby names.

Charlotte and Lucas were almost as obnoxious. With Charlotte's announcement about her pregnancy, Lucas would barely let her out of his sight.

Dexter piled another log on the fire to keep it going, while the girls who'd taken refuge at Hawk's Landing decorated cookies in the kitchen.

But someone was missing.

Two people—Mila and Izzy.

His mother pushed a coffee in his hands. "I know it's difficult, son. You love her, don't you?"

Apparently his poker face only worked in the courtroom. He was as transparent as glass around his family.

"It doesn't matter. She doesn't love me."

His mother made a low sound in her throat. "Don't tell me you believe that."

He shrugged. "I told her how I felt and she said nothing. No, wait, she did. She left."

"She left to protect her little girl."

"I know that, and I love Izzy, too. I could have protected them both."

"Men." His mother rolled her eyes. "Mila left *because* she loves you."

"What?" That made no sense.

"Mila is loving and kind and donates her time to help kids and families. Do you think she would have stayed if being here endangered our family or you?"

Brayden rubbed a hand over his eyes. "No, but—"

"Go after her," his mother said. "She wanted to protect you and us. I heard her talking to Charlotte before she left."

Emotions welled in his throat. Was she right? Did Mila love him?

"But, Mom, I can't leave my job and you. I know how hard it was when you lost Chrissy and then Dad—"

His mother gripped his hands and turned him to look at her. "We all had a difficult time. But one thing I learned from all of it is that when you love someone, you have to show them. You have to treasure every moment you have with them." She kissed his cheek. "You and your brothers are awesome men, Brayden. I'm so proud of you I could burst. That means I want you to be happy."

Brayden swallowed hard.

"Mila and Izzy need you." She gestured toward the kitchen, where the girls had burst into Christmas carols. "I'll be fine. And one day when the danger is over, you'll all come back to us."

Brayden sucked in a breath. "I love you, Mom." He kissed her on the cheek, then gave her a heartfelt hug.

He headed toward Lucas to tell him to arrange for him to join Mila and Izzy.

He just hoped his mother was right and that Mila wanted him.

He motioned to Lucas that they needed to talk. Dexter and Harrison followed them onto the deck with tumblers of whiskey.

Then Brayden explained his decision.

Lucas shook his head. "We can't let you do that," Lucas said.

"Do you know where she is?" Brayden asked.

"No." Lucas sighed.

"Then find out," Brayden said. "You never should have talked her into this without consulting with me."

"It was Mila's choice," Lucas said. "She came to me, Brayden."

"Because she wanted to protect us," Brayden said. "But she's dealing with all this alone, and that's not right."

Lucas offered him an understanding smile, then held up a warning hand. "Listen. We have a lead on DiSanti. I got a call last night. I'm heading out to track him down."

"I'm going with you," Brayden said.

Harrison squared his shoulders. "He messed with my town. I'm in, too."

Dexter shrugged. "Might as well make it four."

Lucas hesitated, then nodded.

Brayden's heart raced. The Hawk men always stuck together. If anyone could stop DiSanti, once and for all, it was them.

Chapter Twenty-Five

Brayden was anxious to get DiSanti.

Harrison met with Jorge to offer protection and arrange for him to be reunited with his family. With Lucas's connections, they'd already struck a deal to help the man get citizenship.

Brayden and Lucas traveled to the property Corley owned in Juarez. Internet chatter revealed that a large merchandise shipment was about to be transported across the border, confirming the information Jorge had supplied. Dexter was headed to a second location they suspected was used to house more victims.

Lucas called for backup when they arrived in Juarez, and they met two teams of agents on the outskirts of the compound.

"I wish you'd stay back," Lucas told Brayden. "Let us handle this, brother."

Normally, Brayden would do exactly that. But this time, he had a personal stake in the case. And he wanted to have his brother's back. After all, Lucas was going to be a father.

And he wanted to see DiSanti locked up, or dead,

himself. It was the only way to free Mila and Izzy so they could come out of hiding and have a normal life.

If they failed today though, he would join her in WITSEC. He hadn't slept a single night for wondering where she was, if she and Izzy were okay, if DiSanti might have found them. The only way he'd know she was safe was to be with her. They'd face the danger and uncertainty together.

Lucas parked a mile from the compound, a large ranch fenced with barbed wire and only a couple of miles from the border. Armed and ready, they hiked on foot until they reached the property. He and Lucas went one direction while Harrison and Dexter joined another team. They split up to approach from different angles.

Gunshots came out of nowhere, and Lucas and Brayden returned fire, taking two guards out. They slipped past the dead guards, snatching their semiautomatic weapons to use if they ran out of ammunition.

The next half hour all hell broke loose. Brayden and Lucas and the teams charged the compound. A helicopter dropped in reinforcements, and they stormed the property.

A bullet clipped his arm as he inched down a long corridor inside the main structure, but he shook off the sting and ducked into a room. Empty.

Lucas's voice echoed from the mike. "Team A located the merchandise. A storage container on the property. Ten girls. Jade was one of them. They were about to be forced through an underground tunnel that crosses into Mexico."

"Any sign of DiSanti?"

Static echoed back. Then gunfire.

Brayden's heart pounded. "Lucas?"

Silence.

Dammit, had Lucas been shot?

"Talk to me, man."

More gunfire. Shouts. Then a low grunt.

Brayden took off running. He couldn't lose his brother.

MILA SMILED AS Izzy added sprinkles to the cookies they'd just baked. A dollop of icing dotted her cheek, and she reached up and wiped it away with one finger.

"I think you have as much on you as you have on the cookies," she said with a laugh.

Izzy licked a gob of sprinkles and icing from her hand. "Yummy!"

Mila laughed and set the second tray in front of her daughter. They had enough cookies for a party.

But it was just the two of them.

"Can we get a tree, Mommy?" Izzy asked.

Mila glanced at the tiny house they'd rented. It was satisfactory, but nothing about it spelled home. They hadn't brought anything with them except clothes and a few of Izzy's toys.

A Christmas tree would at least make the house feel festive. "Of course we'll get a tree. I saw a tree farm in town. We'll go pick out one later and buy some decorations."

"Yippee!" Izzy bounced up and down, and Mila hugged her.

Izzy deserved a happy holiday with Christmas cookies and decorations and Santa Claus.

"Mommy?"

"What, sweetie?"

"Is Santa going to bring me that puppy?"

"We'll see." Maybe they'd visit a rescue shelter later, too, and Izzy could pick out a dog. A pet would be good company for both of them.

Mila looked out the window again at the fresh falling snow. It was beautiful, but she missed Texas and her work.

Most of all, she missed Brayden.

BRAYDEN RACED THROUGH the compound, dodging bullets from two more goons. He found Lucas outside at the back of the compound near a hangar, where he spotted DiSanti's private plane.

Lucas stood, hands raised in surrender as two men pointed guns at him. One of them was DiSanti.

"I'll find her," DiSanti said. "And I'll get my child back."

"Why?" Lucas barked. "So you can sell her like you do other people's children?"

DiSanti motioned to one of his goons, the one with the gun on Lucas. "Kill him, and let's get out of here."

Brayden went cold inside. He refused to lose his brother to this monster. DiSanti had already destroyed too many lives.

He moved slightly so Lucas could see him, then held up three fingers, counting down.

When he reached zero, he aimed a shot at DiSanti's head. Lucas whipped around and punched the goon with the gun, and they fought.

Brayden's bullet hit its mark, the center of DiSanti's

forehead. Blood and brains splattered as the bastard collapsed to the ground.

A gunshot blasted the air, and he jerked his head back to Lucas and the man on the ground. His heart raced. Lucas?

His brother rolled off the shooter, checked the man's pulse, then looked over his shoulder at Brayden.

Thank God. Lucas wasn't hit.

Lucas shoved the man's gun aside, then stood and walked over to DiSanti.

Brayden breathed a sigh of relief when Lucas gave him a smile of approval.

DiSanti was finally dead.

He could go after Mila and bring her home.

MILA DRAGGED IN the Christmas tree, shaking snow from her boots. Colorado was beautiful but cold.

Izzy's teeth chattered.

"I'll make us some hot chocolate," Mila said. Although first she wanted to make certain they hadn't been followed. All day she'd had the strangest feeling that someone was watching her. She'd especially sensed it at the Christmas tree lot.

Izzy ran in, yanking off her gloves, hat and coat, then raced toward the bag of decorations they'd picked up at the thrift store.

Mila hurried back to the door to close it. A dark SUV pulled into the drive, sending fear through her.

Had DiSanti found her?

She started to scream at Izzy to run and hide, but the driver's door opened, and a man emerged. Not DiSanti.

A tall dark-haired cowboy in a Stetson, boots and jeans and a long Western duster coat.

Her heart flip-flopped in her chest.

Brayden.

But fear followed. Was he here to tell her that she and Izzy had to move again?

She opened the door, soaking in the sight of him as he climbed the steps.

A slow smile curved his mouth as his gaze met hers.

"Brayden?"

"He's dead."

Relief nearly knocked her off her feet. "When? What happened?" Heart racing, she stepped onto the porch. "Never mind. I don't care. I'm just glad you're here." She couldn't help herself. She'd missed him so much, she threw her arms around him.

He swept her into a hug and growled in her ear. "I love you, Mila. I want you and Izzy to come home with me."

Love swelled inside her, and she lifted her head to look into his eyes. "I love you, too, Brayden."

"You do?"

Her pulse hammered. "I do."

"Then you'll marry me?" The tentative look in his eyes warmed her heart even more. Did he really expect her to say no?

She slid her arms under his and wrapped them around him. "Yes, I would love to marry you," she whispered.

They both laughed, then their lips fused for a tender, passionate kiss. Seconds later, Izzy squealed and joined them. She wiggled in between them, and they all hugged, then Brayden scooped her up.

"Izzy, I want to marry your mommy, is that okay?"

She bobbed her head up and down, her eyes bright with laughter.

"That means that you'll live with me," Brayden said. "I'd like to be your daddy, too."

"Yes, yes, I want you as my daddy!" She giggled and wrapped her little arms around his neck. When she finally pulled away, she looked over at Mila.

"Santa came early, Mommy."

Mila rubbed her daughter's back. "What do you mean?"

"I tolded you I asked Santa for something else."

Mila smiled. "Yes?"

"I asked him to bring me a daddy of my own!" Izzy squealed. "And he did!"

Tears pricked the back of Mila's eyelids. Izzy and she would have a family now with Brayden at Hawk's Landing.

Santa would also make all of Izzy's wishes come true. Not only would she get a puppy, but she'd get a pony. Blondie would be hers forever.

* * * * *

Look for the final book in USA TODAY *bestselling author Rita Herron's Badge of Justice miniseries,* Hostage at Hawk's Landing, *coming soon.*

And don't miss the previous books in the series:

Redemption at Hawk's Landing
Safe at Hawk's Landing

Available now from Harlequin Intrigue!

SPECIAL EXCERPT FROM

HQN™

*When wealthy cattleman Callen Laramie is called
back home to Coldwater, Texas, for a Christmas
wedding, he has no idea just how much his
attendance will matter to his family...and to the
woman who's never been far from his thoughts—or
his heart.*

Read on for a sneak preview of
Lone Star Christmas
by USA TODAY *bestselling author*
Delores Fossen.

CHAPTER ONE

DEAD STUFFED THINGS just didn't scream Christmas wedding invitation for Callen Laramie. Even when the dead stuffed thing—an armadillo named Billy—was draped with gold tinsel, a bridal veil and was holding a bouquet of what appeared to be tiny poinsettias in his little armadillo hands.

Then again, when the bride-to-be, Rosy Muldoon, was a taxidermist, Callen supposed a photo like that hit the more normal range of possibilities for invitation choices.

Well, normal-ish anyway.

No one had ever accused Rosy of being conventional, and even though he hadn't seen her in close to fourteen years, Billy's bridal picture was proof that her nonnormalcy hadn't changed during that time.

Dragging in a long breath that Callen figured he might need, he opened the invitation. What was printed inside wasn't completely unexpected, not really, but he was glad he'd taken that breath. Like most invitations, it meant he'd have to do something, and doing something like this often meant trudging through the past.

Y'all are invited to the wedding of Buck McCall
and Rosy Muldoon. Christmas Eve at Noon in
the Lightning Bug Inn on Main Street, Coldwater, Texas. Reception to follow.

So, Buck had finally popped the question, and Rosy
had accepted. Again, no surprise. Not on the surface
anyway, since Buck had started "courting" Rosy several
years after both of them had lost their spouses about a
decade and a half ago.

But Callen still got a bad feeling about this.

The bad feeling went up a notch when he saw that
the printed RSVP at the bottom had been lined through
and the words handwritten there. "Please come. Buck
needs to see you. Rosy."

Yes, this would require him to do something.

She'd underlined the *please* and the *needs*, and it was
just as effective as a heavyweight's punch to Callen's
gut. One that knocked him into a time machine and took
him back eighteen years. To that time when he'd first
laid eyes on Buck and then on Rosy shortly thereafter.

Oh man.

Callen had just turned fourteen, and the raw anger
and bad memories had been eating holes in him. Sometimes, they still did. Buck had helped with that. Heck,
maybe Rosy had, too, but the four mostly good years
he'd spent with Buck couldn't erase the fourteen awful
ones that came before them.

He dropped the invitation back on his desk and
steeled himself up when he heard the woodpecker taps
of high heels coming toward his office. Several taps

later, his assistant, Havana Mayfield, stuck her head in the open doorway.

Today, her hair was pumpkin orange with streaks of golden brown, the color of a roasted turkey. Probably to coordinate with Thanksgiving, since it'd been just the day before.

Callen wasn't sure what coordination goal Havana had been going for with the lime-green pants and top or the lipstick-red stilettos, but as he had done with Rosy and just about everyone else from his past, he'd long since given up trying to figure out his assistant's life choices. Havana was an efficient workaholic, like him, which meant he overlooked her wardrobe, her biting sarcasm and the occasional judgmental observations about him—even if they weren't any of her business.

"Your two o'clock is here," Havana said, setting some contracts and more mail in his inbox. Then she promptly took the stack from his outbox. "George Niedermeyer," she added, and bobbled her eyebrows. "He brought his mother with him. She wants to tell you about her grand-daughter, the lawyer."

Great.

Callen silently groaned. George was in his sixties and was looking for a good deal on some Angus. Which Callen could and would give him. George's mother, Myrtle, was nearing ninety, and despite her advanced age, she was someone Callen would classify as a woman with too much time on her hands. Myrtle would try to do some matchmaking with her lawyer granddaughter, gossip about things that Callen didn't want to hear and prolong what should be a half-hour meeting into an hour or more.

"Myrtle said you're better looking than a litter of fat spotted pups," Havana added, clearly enjoying this. "That's what you get for being a hotshot cattle broker with a pretty face." She poked her tongue against her cheek. "Women just can't resist you and want to spend time with you. The older ones want to fix you up with their offspring."

"You've had no trouble resisting," he pointed out— though he'd never made a play for her. And wouldn't. Havana and anyone else who worked for him was genderless as far as Callen was concerned.

"Because I know the depths of your cold, cold heart. Plus, you pay me too much to screw this up for sex with a hotshot cattle broker with a pretty face."

Callen didn't even waste a glare on that. The *pretty face* was questionable, but he was indeed a hotshot cattle broker. That wasn't ego. He had the bank account, the inventory and the willing buyers to prove it.

Head 'em up, move 'em out.

Callen had built Laramie Cattle on that motto. That and plenty of ninety-hour workweeks. And since his business wasn't broke, it didn't require fixing. Even if it would mean having to listen to Myrtle for the next hour.

"What the heck is that?" Havana asked, tipping her head to his desk.

Callen followed her gaze to the invitation. "Billy, the Armadillo. Years ago, he was roadkill."

Every part of Havana's face went aghast. "Ewww."

He agreed, even though he would have gone for something more manly sounding, like maybe a grunt. "The bride's a taxidermist," he added. Along with being Buck's housekeeper and cook.

Still in the aghast mode, Havana shifted the files to her left arm so she could pick up the invitation and open it. He pushed away another greasy smear of those old memories while she read it.

"Buck McCall," Havana muttered when she'd finished.

She didn't ask who he was. No need. Havana had sent Buck Christmas gifts during the six years that she'd worked for Callen. Considering those were the only personal gifts he'd ever asked her to buy and send to anyone, she knew who Buck was. Or rather she knew that he was important to Callen.

Of course, that "important" label needed to be judged on a curve because Callen hadn't actually visited Buck or gone back to Coldwater since he'd hightailed it out of there on his eighteenth birthday. Now he was here in Dallas, nearly three hundred miles away, and sometimes it still didn't feel nearly far enough. There were times when the moon would have been too close.

Havana just kept on staring at him, maybe waiting for him to bare his soul or something. He wouldn't. No reason for it either. Because she was smart and efficient, she had almost certainly done internet searches on Buck. There were plenty of articles about him being a foster father.

Correction: the hotshot of foster fathers.

It wouldn't have taken much for Havana to piece together that Buck had fostered not only Callen but his three brothers, as well. Hell, for that matter Havana could have pieced together the rest, too. The bad stuff that'd happened before Callen and his brothers had gotten to Buck's. Too much for him to stay, though his

brothers had had no trouble putting down those pro-
verbial roots in Coldwater.

"Christmas Eve, huh?" Havana questioned. "You've
already got plans to go to that ski lodge in Aspen with a
couple of your clients. Heck, you scheduled a business
meeting for Christmas morning, one that you insisted I
attend. Say, is Bah Humbug your middle name?"

"The meeting will finish in plenty of time for you to
get in some skiing and spend your Christmas bonus,"
he grumbled. Then he rethought that. "Do you ski?"

She lifted her shoulder. "No, but there are worse
things than sitting around a lodge during the holidays
while the interest on my bonus accumulates in my in-
vestment account."

Yes, there were worse things. And Callen had some
firsthand experience with that.

"Are you actually thinking about going back to Coldwater for this wedding?" Havana pressed.

"No." But he was sure thinking about the wedding
itself and that note Rosy had added to the invitation.

Please.

That wasn't a good word to have repeating in his
head.

Havana shrugged and dropped the invitation back
on his desk. "Want me to send them a wedding gift?
Maybe they've registered on the Taxidermists-R-Us
site." Her tongue went in her cheek again.

Callen wasted another glare on her and shook his
head. "I'll take care of it. I'll send them something."

She staggered back, pressed her folder-filled hand
to her chest. "I think the earth just tilted on its axis. Or
maybe that was hell freezing over." Havana paused,

looked at him. "Is something wrong?" she came out and asked, her tone no longer drenched with sarcasm.

Callen dismissed it by motioning toward the door. "Tell the Niedermeyers that I need a few minutes. I have to do something first."

As expected, that caused Havana to raise an eyebrow again, and before she left, Callen didn't bother to tell her that her concern wasn't warranted. He could clear this up with a phone call and get back to work.

But who should he call?

Buck was out because if there was actually something wrong, then his former foster father would be at the center of it. That *Please come. Buck needs to see you* clued him into that.

He scrolled through his contacts, one by one. He no longer had close friends in Coldwater, but every now and then he ran into someone in his business circles who passed along some of that gossip he didn't want to hear. So the most obvious contacts were his brothers.

Kace, the oldest, was the town's sheriff. Callen dismissed talking to him because the last time they'd spoken—four or five years ago—Kace had tried to lecture Callen about cutting himself off from the family. Damn right, he'd cut himself off, and since he would continue to do that and hated lectures from big brothers, he went to the next one.

Judd. Another big brother who was only a year older than Callen. Judd had been a cop in Austin. Or maybe San Antonio. He was a deputy now in Coldwater, but not once had he ever bitched about Callen leaving the "fold." He kept Judd as a possibility for the call he needed to make and continued down the very short list to consider the rest of his choices.

Nico. The youngest brother, who Callen almost immediately discounted. He was on the rodeo circuit—a bull rider of all things—and was gone a lot. He might not have a clue if something was wrong.

Callen got to Rosy's name next. The only reason she was in his contacts was because Buck had wanted him to have her number in case there was an emergency. A *please* on a wedding invitation probably didn't qualify as one, but since he hated eating up time by waffling, Callen pressed her number. After a couple of rings, he got her voice mail.

"Knock knock," Rosy's perky voice greeted, and she giggled like a loon. "Who's there? Well, obviously not me, and since Billy can't answer the phone, ha ha, you gotta leave me a message. Talk sweet to me, and I'll talk sweet back." More giggling as if it were a fine joke.

Callen didn't leave a message because a) he wanted an answer now and b) he didn't want anyone interrupting his day by calling him back.

He scrolled back through the contacts and pressed Judd's number. Last he'd heard, Judd had moved into the cabin right next to Buck's house, so he would know what was going on.

"Yes, it came from a chicken's butt," Judd growled the moment he answered. "Now, get over it and pick it up."

In the background Callen thought he heard someone make an *ewww* sound eerily similar to the one Havana had made earlier. Since a chicken's butt didn't have anything to do with a phone call or wedding invitation, it made Callen think his brother wasn't talking to him.

"What the heck do you want?" Judd growled that, too, and this time Callen did believe he was on the receiving end of the question.

The bad grouchy attitude didn't bother Callen because he thought it might speed along the conversation. Maybe. Judd didn't like long personal chats, which explained why they rarely talked.

"Can somebody else gather the eggs?" a girl asked. Callen suspected it might be the same one who'd ewww'ed. Her voice was high-pitched and whiny. "These have poop on them."

"This is a working ranch," Judd barked. "There's poop everywhere. If you've got a gripe with your chores, talk to Buck or Rosy."

"They're not here," the whiner whined.

"There's Shelby," Judd countered. "Tell her all about it and quit bellyaching to me."

Just like that, Callen got another ass-first knock back into the time machine. Shelby McCall. Buck's daughter. And the cause of nearly every lustful thought that Callen had had from age fifteen all the way through to age eighteen.

Plenty of ones afterward, too.

Forbidden fruit could do that to a teenager, and as Buck's daughter, Shelby had been as forbidden as it got. Callen remembered that Buck had had plenty of rules, but at the top of the list was one he gave to the boys he fostered. *Touch Shelby, and I'll castrate you.* It had been simple and extremely effective.

"Buck got a new batch of foster kids," Judd went on,

and again, Callen thought that part of the conversation was meant for him. "I just finished a double shift, and I'm trying to get inside my house so I can sleep, but I keep getting bothered. What do you want?" he tacked onto that mini-rant.

"I got Buck and Rosy's wedding invitation," Callen threw out there.

"Yeah. Buck popped the question a couple of weeks ago, and they're throwing together this big wedding deal for Christmas Eve. They're inviting all the kids Buck has ever fostered. All of them," Judd emphasized. "So, no, you're not special and didn't get singled out because you're a stinkin' rich prodigal son. *All of them*," he repeated.

Judd sounded as pleased about that as Callen would have been had he still been living there. He had no idea why someone would want to take that kind of step back into the past. It didn't matter that Buck had been good to them. The only one who had been. It was that being there brought back all the stuff that'd happened before they'd made it to Buck.

"Is Buck okay?" Callen asked.

"Of course he is," Judd snapped. Then he paused. "Why wouldn't he be? Just gather the blasted eggs!" he added onto that after another whiny *ewww*. "Why wouldn't Buck be okay?"

Callen didn't want to explain the punch-in-the-gut feeling he'd gotten with Rosy's *Please come. Buck needs to see you*, and it turned out that he didn't have to explain it.

"Here's Shelby, thank God," Judd grumbled before Callen had to come up with anything. "She'll answer any questions you have about the wedding. It's Callen," he said to Shelby. "Just leave my phone on the porch when you're done."

"No!" Callen couldn't say it fast enough. "That's all right. I was just—"

"Callen," Shelby greeted.

Apparently, his lustful thoughts weren't a thing of the past after all. Even though Shelby was definitely a woman now, she could still purr his name.

He got a flash image of her face. Okay, of her body, too. All willowy and soft with that tumble of blond hair and clear green eyes. And her mouth. Oh man. That mouth had always had his number.

"I didn't expect you to be at Judd's," he said, not actually fishing for information. But he was. He was also trying to fight back what appeared to be jealousy. It was something he didn't feel very often.

"Oh, I'm not. I was over here at Dad's, taking care of a few things while he's at an appointment. He got some new foster kids in, and when I heard the discussion about eggs, I came outside. That's when Judd handed me his phone and said I had to talk to you. You got the wedding invitation?" she asked.

"I did." He left it at that, hoping she'd fill in the blanks of the questions he wasn't sure how to ask.

"We couldn't change Rosy's mind about using that picture of Billy in the veil. Trust me, we tried."

Callen found himself smiling. A bad combination when mixed with arousal. Still, he could push it aside, and he did that by glancing around his office. He had every nonsexual thing he wanted here, and if he wanted sex, there were far less complicated ways than going after Shelby. Buck probably still owned at least one good castrating knife.

"I called Rosy, but she didn't answer," Callen explained.

"She's in town but should be back soon. She doesn't answer her phone if she's driving."

Callen couldn't decide if that was a good or bad thing on a personal level for him. If Rosy had answered, then he wouldn't be talking to Shelby right now. He wouldn't feel the need for a cold shower or an explanation.

"Rosy should be back any minute now. You want me to have her call you?" Shelby asked.

"No. I just wanted to tell them best wishes for the wedding. I'll send a gift and a card." And he'd write a personal note to Buck.

"You're not coming?" Shelby said.

Best to do this fast and efficient. "No. I have plans. Business plans. A trip. I'll be out of the state." And he cursed himself for having to justify himself to a woman who could lead to castration.

"Oh."

That was it. Two letters of the alphabet. One word. But it was practically drowning in emotion. Exactly what specific emotion, Callen didn't know, but that gut-punch feeling went at him again hard and fast.

"Shelby?" someone called out. It sounded like the whiny girl. "Never mind. Here comes Miss Rosy."

"I guess it's an important business trip?" Shelby continued, her voice a whisper now.

"Yes, longtime clients. I do this trip with them every year—"

"Callen, you need to come," Shelby interrupted. "Soon," she added. "It's bad news."

* * * * *

Don't miss
Lone Star Christmas *by Delores Fossen,*
available now wherever
HQN Books and ebooks are sold.

www.HQNBooks.com

It all began with a kiss. At least that was the way Chloe Clementine remembered it. A winter kiss, which is nothing like a summer one. The cold, icy air around you. Puffs of white breaths intermingling. Warm lips touching, tingling as they meet for the very first time.

Chloe thought that kiss would be the last thing she remembered before she died of old age. It was the kiss—and the cowboy who'd kissed her—that she'd been dreaming about when her phone rang. Being in Whitehorse had brought it all back after all these years.

She groaned, wanting to keep sleeping so she could stay in that cherished memory longer. Her phone rang again. She swore that if it was one of her sisters calling this early…

"What?" she demanded into the phone without bothering to see who was calling. She was so sure that it would be her youngest sister, Annabelle, the morning person.

"Hello?" The voice was male and familiar. For just a moment she thought she'd conjured up the cowboy from the kiss. "It's Justin."

Justin? She sat straight up in bed. Thoughts zipped past at a hundred miles an hour. How had he gotten her cell phone number? Why was he calling? Was he in Whitehorse?

"Justin," she said, her voice sounding croaky from sleep. She cleared her throat. "I thought it was Annabelle calling. What's up?" She glanced at the clock. *What's up at seven forty-five in the morning?*

"I know it's early but I got your message."

Now she really was confused. "My message?" She had danced with his best friend at the Christmas dance recently, but she hadn't sent Justin a message.

"That you needed to see me? That it was urgent?"

She had no idea what he was talking about. Had her sister Annabelle done this? She couldn't imagine her sister Tessa Jane doing such a thing. But since her sisters had fallen in love they hadn't been themselves.

"I'm sorry, but I didn't send you a message. You're sure it was from me?"

"The person calling just told me that you were in trouble and needed my help. There was loud music in the background as if whoever it was might have called me from a bar."

He didn't think she'd drunk-dialed him, did he? "Sorry, but it wasn't me." She was more sorry than he knew. "And I can't imagine who would have called you on my behalf." Like the devil, she couldn't. It had to be her sister Annabelle.

"Well, I'm glad to hear that you aren't in trouble and urgently need my help," he said, not sounding like that at all.

She closed her eyes, now wishing she'd made something up. What was she thinking? She didn't need to improvise. She was in trouble, though nothing urgent exactly. At least for the moment.

Don't miss
Rugged Defender *by B.J. Daniels,*
available November 2018 wherever
Harlequin® Intrigue books and ebooks are sold.

www.Harlequin.com

Need an adrenaline rush from nail-biting tales
(and irresistible males)?

Check out **Harlequin Intrigue**®
and **Harlequin**® **Romantic Suspense** books!

New books available every month!

CONNECT WITH US AT:

Facebook.com/groups/HarlequinConnection

 Facebook.com/HarlequinBooks

Twitter.com/HarlequinBooks

 Instagram.com/HarlequinBooks

Pinterest.com/HarlequinBooks

ReaderService.com

⬧HARLEQUIN®

**ROMANCE WHEN
YOU NEED IT**

SGENRE2018

Love Harlequin romance?

DISCOVER.

Be the first to find out about promotions,
news and exclusive content!

 Facebook.com/HarlequinBooks

Twitter.com/HarlequinBooks

 Instagram.com/HarlequinBooks

Pinterest.com/HarlequinBooks

ReaderService.com

EXPLORE.

Sign up for the Harlequin e-newsletter and
download a free book from any series at
TryHarlequin.com.

CONNECT.

Join our Harlequin community to share
your thoughts and connect with other
romance readers!
Facebook.com/groups/HarlequinConnection

Reward the book lover in you!

Earn points on your purchase of new Harlequin books from participating retailers.

Turn your points into **FREE BOOKS** of your choice!

Join for FREE today at
www.HarlequinMyRewards.com.

Harlequin My Rewards is a free program (no fees) without any commitments or obligations.

MYR18